I'M LEAVING IT

AND OTHER STORIES

Published by Paul Dore Creative Services. 1 Shaw Street, Suite
316, Toronto, Ontario, Canada, M6K 0A1, pauldore.com.
Cover Design: Ellen Yu.
Book Layout: Paul Dore.

Library and Archives Canada Cataloguing in Publication

Dore, Paul, 1978 - author
I'm Leaving It and Other Stories / Paul Dore.

ISBN 978-1-9994067-4-5 (epub)
ISBN 978-1-7771683-0-8 (kindle)
ISBN 978-1-9994067-9-0 (paperback)

To my mother: I tried really hard not to swear.

CONTENTS

PART ONE: LOVE

LOOKING FOR LOVE IN ALL

THE WRONG PLACES

If it's true - wherever you go, there you are - then I'm in trouble.

The concept of finding a life partner has consistently eluded me. I used to regard this as my own internal dysfunction, and recently, I've made the conscious choice to let people off the hook.

It's not you, it's me.

The expiry date sticker on my relationships reads three years. A person I was chatting with online, after 256 messages, asked about this cap. When I revealed that my longest relationship was three years, she regarded this as reckless and deficient. In all caps, which is the text message equivalent of screaming, she added:" I WOULD RATHER YOU TOLD ME YOUR [sic] MARRIED AND DIVORCED TWICE INSTEAD OF THAT YOUR LONGEST RELATIONSHIP WAS ONLY THREE YEARS." As an aside, she had been in two ten-year relationships in her entire life. So, I guess everyone has their own individualized expiry date.

Let's break this down.

Three years is a reasonable amount of time. A year of the honeymoon period where we're falling in love, actively going out on adventures together and sending text messages too embarrassing to include here. A second year of settling in, settling down. The adventures less, the text messages functional. By the third year, the equation of perpetuating a decision that involved spending the rest of our lives together, plus reproducing miniature versions of us, equals

a shutdown of emotions on my part.
This shutdown was evidence of my inability to just cut and run. To be honest, not a proud fact. No, the tactics I employed included disallowing the other person to truly know who I was on the inside. If I didn't understand my core, how could someone else be expected to interact emotionally with me? This buffer zone of disconnection created a bond between myself and the other person. We both claimed the same problem: we didn't know the real me, the core.
That's usually around the three-year mark.
Roll credits.
I was a good boyfriend and all if you're talking about practical and superficial elements, which only caused a gross imbalance. Usually, the other person in my partnerships met someone else. Maybe this someone else revealed their core quickly, and my partner thought, *Wow, that guy I'm with, Paul, sure is shut down emotionally. This new guy showed me his core right away and without me even asking. See ya, Paul!*
So, really, both me and my partners were doubling down on the 'it's not me, it's you' blame game. On the positive side, at least this was something that brought us together.
It's been a while since my last real relationship, depending on when this book is published. Perhaps between now and then, I will have met someone and currently be in that honeymoon phase. The words written here will seem alien, a relic of a past life that no longer lines up with the current tone of my text messages.
Let's not get ahead of ourselves.
At this time, I am 42 years old. A rough - and generous - calculation of a combined amount of time spent in relationships is twelve years. That means I've spent 30 years as a single person. Okay, the first fifteen years or so of my life

shouldn't be included, but even minus that, #TeamSingle is still winning at fifteen years.

Here's the thing: a bunch of unpleasantries happened over the past couple of years. I almost died, someone important to me died, climate change, etc. I am grateful and privileged to have such supportive friends to be there for me in my time of need. But at the end of the day, they have to go home. There's an advantage with a partner, they know you better than anyone else. Part of a relationship is to experience life together, all the ups and downs. Most of the time, I'm fine, but every once in awhile, I experience extreme pains of loneliness.

My relationship life was at a crossroads. I needed to fix it, and what better way then to bring someone else into this mess? Things would be different this time!

I dropped in and out of online dating with little success. At first, it was fun. I connected with someone through words, met them and spent a few hours with an interesting person. Even if there was no spark, I walked away with a positive experience.

Then the dark times came.

Anyone who ventured into the world of online dating has a fair share of nightmare scenarios. I'll share just one: the time I dated a ghost. I unequivocally don't believe ghosts are real, but they are everywhere.

I met Lucy online, and everything moved innocently along. A red flag should have been when she stole things. Little things, like a bottle of hot sauce at a restaurant. Knives and forks. Something was exciting about Lucy, and so I looked past this.

The late-night phone calls started, the voice on the other end saying her oppressive parents tore her room apart again. I drove across the city to pick Lucy up, hair dishevelled, bruises on her arms. At other times, I'd get the call early in the morning to come to a random apartment complex, telling me she didn't want to talk about it. Telling me, it was nothing.

The real trouble came when Lucy moved in with me. Except for roommates, I'd never really lived with someone. In one of my relationships, my girlfriend lived five minutes away on the other side of a park. The ideal situation. Sure, I was almost always at her place or she at mine. But I took solace in just knowing that if something went down, my apartment was a short jaunt through the park.

And it was a beautiful park.

Anyway.

Back to the ghost.

We went to Lucy's house secretly to get some clothes during the day when her parents weren't home. From the foyer through the window, a car pulled into the driveway behind mine. Damnit, why didn't I park on the street? Blocked. A getaway impossible.

The foyer was small, so when her mother opened the door, I got caught behind it. I did what anyone would do in this situation: I put my hands in the air like she was a cop busting me for breaking and entering. When she found me, a stranger, standing in her foyer with my arms up, I said, "I'm a friend of Lucy's." She didn't flinch, didn't move. Only her eyes narrowed, she saw right through me. Without taking her eyes off me, she called for Lucy and climbed the stairs into the house. They yelled at each other and Lucy appeared, her mother following close behind. Her mother turned to me and said, "Wait outside, I would like to speak to my daughter in private." Lucy stormed down the stairs, and we left. Well, once her mother came out and moved her car, then we made a grand getaway.

At the time, I wasn't myself. I almost got into fights. I've gone my entire life without getting into a fight. We were heading to a restaurant, one of those in a back alley with no sign. Frustrated, we cut through a parking lot. The attendant blocked the way as he backed in a car. He started yelling at me to wait, I yelled back at him to hurry up. He gave me the finger, and I slammed on the hood, yelling, "Hey, I'm walkin' here!"

We'd also get into gloves-off screaming matches, Lucy and I. This is not my way. I'm more of a represser. Why scream at someone when you can shove those things deep down into your gut where they cause cancer? That's how I do things. But, there was something off about her. I wasn't sure what was real and what was made up in her mind.

The last straw came when we met some friends of mine - another couple - for dinner. I had received a gift certificate from one of my students for a fancy restaurant. Lucy informed us that she invited along a friend. He showed up and was not nearly as confused as us. When this guy put his hand on Lucy's thigh, my friend asked him how they knew each other, and he replied, "We met online." I had one of those moments - like a montage of memories in a movie - where I instantly replayed every detail of every situation with Lucy, and it made sense all of a sudden. I asked them to leave, and Lucy flipped out because I was being rude, not wanting to pay for her date's bill. She yelled, "But you've got a gift certificate!" Once they were gone, my friends proceeded to get me throw-down, morning-puke drunk.

Then she disappeared.

Her dating profile deleted, her social media profiles gone. I had no evidence she existed. Therefore, the obvious explanation being that she was a ghost.

So, I swore off online dating, at least for the moment.

I have a pretty active social life. Perhaps I could meet someone with shared interests at one of the many events I frequented? Maybe meeting a person face-to-face would be more effective than profile pic-to-profile pic?

And this did happen.

At a networking event for creatives - I know, sounds terrible - I struck up a conversation with a person that looked as awkward and out of place as me.

The person from the networking for creatives event and I started spending time together. She often talked about the 'jerks' - her words, not mine - that she was dating and how she wished she could meet someone like me. I floated the idea that she had already met someone like me - me.

Sometimes, truthful thoughts should remain as thoughts and not become words.

I suggested we go out on a date. She said, "How about you ask me again tomorrow?" Tomorrow, I messaged her, apologizing if I created an awkward situation.

A few weeks went by, and as a way to continue our friendship, I invited her out to another event - one where people shared stories to a live audience. She was enthusiastic and asked if she could bring this new guy she was dating. I had put myself out there as a potential dating partner, so what a great opportunity for some awkwardness. And of course, I can't help to make comparisons.

Vladimir seemed nice at the beginning. His name wasn't Vladimir, but he was Russian. I have nothing against Russians, some of my best friends are Russian. He wore a baseball cap and a hockey jersey. His physique was similar to mine, but that was where our similarities ended.

The first thing Vladimir did when he sat down was to order a giant plate of ribs. Through the entire event, he either gnawed at the ribs or whispered. Both of those things are number one and number two on my list of what not to do at a live event.

As mentioned, these were oral stories and very intense. A woman talked about how as a child growing up in Afghanistan, she was often stopped by soldiers at gunpoint on her way to school. When I glanced over at Vladimir, he's sucking the meat off a rib bone. A man told us about a civil war erupting in his country and how he saved his little brothers. His story was interrupted two times when Vladimir licked his fingers loudly, timing it right as the storyteller paused for dramatic effect.

When I asked Vladimir what he thought about the stories, he shrugged and said, "I guess it beats staying home and watching tv." *I guess it beats staying home and watching tv.* At that point, due to his complete lack of intellectual or emotional curiosity, I grabbed two bare rib bones and stuffed them up his nostrils. Okay, I didn't, but I really wanted to.

Leaving that night, I thought about what Vladimir had that I didn't. You could really drive yourself insane going down that road. I haven't seen her or Vladimir since that night. So, scratch meeting someone face-to-face at an event.

A friend a bit older than me suggested I might already know my partner in crime, which turned out to be the case for her. Through a social media platform, she reconnected with someone from ten years ago. He asked her to go for coffee, she said yes, now they're together.

Sounds simple.

At around the same time, an ex-girlfriend got in touch with me and wanted to have coffee. This was several years after our relationship ended. We caught up on each other's lives, and I figured this was a one-off meet-up until she called me a few days later.

We had a long sprawling talk, and at the end, she

suggested that perhaps we should get back together. I had not even taken it into consideration, and when I asked her why she thought this was a good idea, she said, "Well, we're both single and getting older. We're running out of options." I didn't think this was a good foundation to build a relationship upon, and I said so.

Sometimes, truthful thoughts should remain as thoughts and not become words. I had not learned my lesson. She did not appreciate my response.

That ex of mine was right - I was running out of options. I shouldn't have, but I watched a movie that I knew would trigger one of my classic emotional downward spirals. It was about a man denying his sexuality, and years later, he reconnected with another man who was the only person he had ever been with in a physically affectionate way. You felt the profound loneliness emanating from his body. As human beings, we need love, both physical and otherwise. The main character wandered through life, feeling like he was unworthy of love. Putting aside people committing heinous acts against others, who is undeserving of love?

Sometimes when I see young people in their 20s, I think: *Take advantage of this fountain of youth and have all the sex you can muster.* When I was that age, I kept looking for *The One*, instead of spending time with *The Many*, learning about how to be an adult with another person. Learn what I wanted, my desires. Experience a life that involved cohabitation.

As I hit my 30s, the inevitable happened - friends around me started getting married, establishing homes, having kids and moving out of the city to the suburbs and small towns. This actually made me angry - this was not us, we were the generation that rejected this migration out of the city, this replacement of our creative dreams with kids. Of course, every generation believes this.

Question: when you find yourself in your 40s, alone, mostly working from home, not affiliated with any church or community centre, long past university - where do you meet new people and, by extension, potential partners? You see, no one really prepares you for this part. Societal norms assume that we are going to grow up, get married and have kids. What if this simply is not in the cards for you?

As you progress from a kid and into college or university or starting work, there is a natural order to meeting others. You're going through something with people. For me, I met a lot of people in university that would continue to be friends until the 30-year-old cut off point. We were all transitioning from awkward high school kids, many of us from sheltered small towns, into know-it-all semi-adults. We loved, fought, got drunk, got high, broke up with people, created work, failed - all in the span of four years. And we did it by living tightly packed together in residence. We formed small armies of like-minded individuals, different from finding friends when you were a kid where the only requirement was proximity.

As these university friends fell away, I found myself quite alone and wondering why I felt terrible about it. I actually enjoy going to events or shows or plays or movies by myself. During this time, I went to see a movie in the theatre every week by myself. I'd go at odd times, and usually, the theatre had a few other lone stragglers. When the lights went down, we were all equal. That good looking couple who walked in with linked arms? Didn't matter. Our collective aloneness didn't matter.

Besides, when you're dealing with another person, you have to deal with someone disrupting your carefully crafted routine. For example, I am never late for anything. I like watching the previews before a movie. I went out on a date, and when arranging a time to meet, she said, "There's no rush, there's like 20 minutes of previews before the movie starts." My reply: "This isn't going to work out." When you go to see a play, they very much frown upon late arrivals. Another time, I sat at the bar outside of the theatre, waiting for a date. When she arrived, she was not even flustered. I mean, be flustered - even a little bit - for show! Instead, she sat down on the stool next to me and ordered a beer. We never did get into the play, and we never went on a date again.

About a year ago, one of those moments happened that made me re-think this entire concept of unrelenting joy in my singleness. I was sitting in my apartment having a glass of wine with a date. She sat on my red couch, glass of red wine in her hand. We were about two glasses in and having a conversation about her job. On the surface, I was charming and inquisitive. Inside, I was on fire. As she liberally held the wine glass in her hand, the liquid sloshed from side to side, threatening to spill. I had to keep reminding myself not to stare. This was what being an adult was all about, sharing your personal space with another and trusting that they would resp-

That's when she spilled the entire glass of red wine on my couch. Sure, it was a red couch, but a different shade of red. I still have the couch, and the stain remains.

A reminder.

I keep the couch - and the stain - as a physical representation of my inability to welcome someone into my life. Perhaps I've just lived by myself too long? The place I've settled in speaks volumes of my desire to forever be alone. There simply is no room for anyone else. A loft is for someone in their late 20s, not a man in his 40s. There's no storage here, so I am constantly convincing myself that I don't need some forlorn historical relic of my past. On the surface, I tell myself it is clutter, and I don't need that sweater I haven't worn since 2007 or that record player that belonged to my parents and doesn't work anymore. Purge it.

With my physical space, I've made a declaration: another person is not welcome here. Even when I have friends over, I have a limited amount of time where I can let go of moisture-laden glasses placed on side tables and crumbs falling from plates on to the floor. After everyone leaves, I obsessively clean and sweep and vacuum. If someone lived with me, the time limit would be infinite, and all my energy would be consumed by gathering each long hair in the tub or making sure the toilet is sparkling. Who wants to live with that guy?

But, society tells me I must find my partner in crime, my better half, my emotional confidante.

Desperation set in. I'm running out of time.

Being in your 40s seems to be when the divorces are happening, which I figured upped my chances, so I re-initialized my online account. I cannot speak to the unfortunate things my female friends have to put up with online. Men generally seem terrible. After messaging with a few people, I started noticing a different trend since my last time online. Messages took on more of an interrogation approach. I get it, especially from the female perspective, they want to figure out if I'm a real person. Still, it could be tedious if you are a real person.

Some quick highlights of exchanges from potential online partners.

Highlight #1:

Her: "If your girlfriend went to the bathroom with the door open, how would you react?"

13

Me: "Depends on two things. First, what stage in the relationship? Second, is it a #1 or #2?"
Highlight #2:
Her: "Have you ever lived with someone?"
Me: "Sort of."
Her: "I've only lived with one person, my ex-husband. I would never live with another person without a cohabitation contract."
Highlight #3:
Her: "What made you become vegetarian? What do you think about gays and lesbians?"
Me: "How are vegetarians and gay and lesbian people related?"
Her: "Obvious, isn't it?"
Me: Delete contact.

This was clearly going nowhere. I finally found someone that was a 94% match and who started her profile with this: *I like roasting beets and baking pie while listening to* This American Life. *You should message me if you care about the state of the world, and you can make me laugh.*

I care very deeply about the state of the world. But I latched on to these two elements: making her laugh and beets. I searched the internet for jokes about the root vegetable beets.

Aside: there are a lot of websites dedicated solely to jokes about vegetables.

So, here is the original message I wrote to an actual person online. Please keep in mind that I acted before really thinking this through.

One day two beets, who were best friends, walked together down the street. They stepped off the curb, and a speeding car came around the corner and ran one of them over. The uninjured beet called 911 and helped his injured friend as best he was able. The injured beet was taken to emergency at the hospital and rushed into surgery. After a long and agonizing wait, the doctor finally appeared. He told the uninjured beet, "I have good news, and I have bad news. The good news is that your friend is going to pull through. The bad news is that he's going to be a vegetable for the rest of his life."

- What can I say, I like a good beet joke.

I've neither heard nor told a beet joke in my life. The things we do for love. Once I hit send, and saw this as a sent message and imagined being the person on the other side, receiving this on their computer or phone, I immediately deleted my account.

The plan now is to 'work on myself,' which essentially means I'm doomed to live out the rest of my days alone, eventually getting old, then older and dying in my apartment where I'm found bloated days later by neighbours I never spoke to since they moved in five years previously.

As my editor says, "Always end on a positive note!" Mission accomplished.

THE KöLN CONCERT

Music is a transportation device. Not an original idea, I know, but true. It's an easy topic to write about - sad songs that lyrically extrapolate lost love and heartbreak. Catchy tunes that conveniently fit into a three-minute song.

Not me, no. When I think of heartbreak, I think of a twenty-six-minute contemporary improvised piece of piano music recorded in 1975. It was a simpler time back then, mostly because I was not born yet.

In my mid-twenties, I was in a relationship with a woman that lasted about two years. Made it just under the three-year expiry date. It just sort of fizzled out, and I can only speculate that when confronted with the concept of a life with me, this person got a reality check. Speculation, of course. I don't know what was going on in her head. Near the beginning, she looked at my book collection and said, "Not a lot of women on those shelves." Maybe this was the reason? Her ability to get right to it. She did have a point, and since then, I've tried to be better at gender balancing my books.

Desperation on my part could have been the reason it ended. I brought a box of her stuff from my place to hers. We hugged, I hoped she'd change her mind. Spoiler alert: she didn't.

Anyway.

The point is we didn't last. There is a silver lining in this heartbreak: 'The Köln Concert.' Are we not a collection of likes and dislikes based on what we learn in relationships with others?

After living alone for a while, I wanted music in my life. Not to be in a band or play for people, just for me. As a teenager, my parents shipped me off to piano lessons once a week. This wasn't my favourite thing to do at the time. My teacher was almost completely blind, and her husband was totally blind. The lessons took place at her house and the husband - a tall man with hair that stood on end like he received a shock on the second floor - always lumbered down the stairs to greet the students.

The piano was in the basement, and the teacher began by asking me if I practiced during the week. She saw through my lies. When she needed to see something on the page, she used a giant magnifying glass, having to lean over my shoulder, getting her face right up to the music notes. She did this often because usually, I played the wrong notes, confusing the hell out of her.

At the end of every lesson, she played a piece of music. It was incredible and all from memory. At the same time, it made my heart swell and discouraged me from ever believing I could play like her.

Here's a lesson for all the kids out there: learn to play an instrument. Years later, I appreciated that I could read music. Sure, it was a pain in the ass at the time, but you'll thank me later on in life.

I secretly wanted to play the guitar. In the 1990s, when I discovered the Pearl Jam album *Ten*, I listened to only those eleven songs for at least a year. Most young men have dreams of being a rock star, but the reason why I wanted to be in a band was that they got to wear whatever they wanted. A grown man wearing a plaid shirt, jeans and sneakers to work? Sign me up.

This dream remained a dream. I was never in any bands - I don't work well with others. Figured we'd get into fights over who was the frontman, the drummer would sleep with the bass player's girlfriend, we'd argue about whether to sell out when the offers came from the record companies and so on.

Years later, when I was an adult, I decided to buy myself a guitar. I was producing a movie and wrote into the script that one of the characters always carried around a guitar, so I could write off the expense as being a prop. There was a scene where the character got mad and ripped the strings off the guitar. The actor went all method and wanted to smash the guitar like Pete Townshend from The Who, but I insisted this was 'out of character.'

The guitar was difficult to wrangle. I brought in a musician friend to help re-string it and said, "I'm having a difficult time reaching my left hand around the neck." He took one look at the guitar and said, "This is a classical guitar; the neck is wider. Dummy." I didn't think he needed to add the dummy part. Maybe he didn't, but that's what I heard. He was the expert, after all. He helped me string up the guitar and left me to it.

To learn chords and frets, I was using online guitar lessons. After going through a few of these programs, I noticed that many of the songs they used were religious, like 'Michael Row the Boat Ashore' or 'Amazing Grace.' Where were all the secular guitar lessons?

Practicing 'Michael Row the Boat Ashore' one day, I heard a creaking as though I was in the hull of a ship in a storm. The creaking intensified, and one of the guitar strings snapped, striking me on the left cheek. The creaking continued, another string snapped, just missing my eye. I threw the guitar across the room, and as it crashed to the floor, the remaining strings snapped and cracked like fireworks. My musician friend had strung them too tight. Dummy.

After my guitar attacked me, I retired from the instrument. I still have that guitar, but now it's just decoration. A conversation piece: "Oh, you play the guitar?" Me: "Well, no, I quit playing after my guitar attacked me." Great first line.

But I still wanted music in my life.

A few more years went by, and I finally bought myself a keyboard. Reading music really is like riding a bike. I found sheet music for 'The Köln Concert' and decided I was going to learn how to play it, a page at a time. The first problem: the piece is 87 pages long. The second problem: it's incredibly complex.

But it's all about the journey, right? It's not like I was planning on playing this live for an audience.

On January 24th, 1975, jazz and classical pianist Keith Jarrett performed 'The Köln Concert.' The concert was completely improvised, and as Jarrett said, "The music played should go as quickly as it comes." The subsequent album went on to become the biggest selling jazz album in history and the all-time best selling piano album. Jarrett is known as a very physical player, meaning you can hear him on the recordings grunting and humming along, and he almost seemed to be dancing on the piano bench. The concept of the concert was for him to step on stage with no notes in his head and make the music up entirely in the moment.

To this day, I still pull out this concert. For me, he accomplished what he set out to do. At the beginning, you can hear hints of themes and melodies, but most of the piece is searching around for what to play. The music gets dark, lighter, dark again. Near the end, you can hear when all of the searching comes together, erupting into a rapturous conclusion.

After a week, I was on page 2. There's stuff going on in there that I had to go back into musical theory to figure out.

Page 2 after a week. Took Jarret about an hour to make the whole thing up.

Why am I obsessed with 'The Köln Concert'? I'm sure some people would listen to it and think: *This isn't even music*. But there's something to it. Maybe it's Jarrett's voice humming along? Him banging on the piano? Maybe it's when you can hear in the music a searching for some kind of theme, some kind of something, and you can hear it in his voice when he hits it, when everything comes together?

There's an imperfect humanity about the piece. Jarrett just sat down with a blank mind and did what is so amazing about musicians, about art, hell, about human beings - he created something out of nothing. Where there was only dead air, he filled it with disparate notes, the audience/listener and the player not sure if this was going to work, not sure whether this was all going to make something coherent. Isn't that the point? To make something that exists in a moment, something shared between people and that connects them to the creative spirit? It speaks to me in a way that represents the mystery of creativity - where does it come from? How and when is an idea born? How does it evolve?

When I hear 'The Köln Concert,' it doesn't matter, I don't have these questions, it is just something that exists, and it makes me feel. It takes me to a place that is far away from existence as I know it to be, yet is organic and natural like it came from beneath the dirt of Earth itself.

Playing 'The Köln Concert' through my own fingers transported me back to thinking about the ex-girlfriend that introduced me to it. Not in a way where I wished to win her back. After more than a decade, we're both different people. It was also not a wish to be back in that time with her. It was more of an appreciation of our time together. How fortunate can one person be to have, if even for a limited amount of time, a joining with another who teaches them things and makes them a better person?

Above I said I just wanted music in my life for myself, not to play for others. I lied. After working through 'The Köln Concert,' I wanted to share it with others. So, I arranged a small concert in my apartment for three friends of mine. I even provided light snacks and refreshing beverages of the alcohol variety. Want to get people to indulge you in playing a piano concert for them in your apartment? Provide light snacks and refreshing beverages of the alcohol variety.

My goal was to accurately re-create the concert. Let me say this upfront: the playing was terrible. But in addition to playing (mostly) right notes, I banged on the keyboard whenever Jarrett did, cried out in ecstasy. As I got deeper into the piece, my body and mind were completely transported to a different place and time.

Transported to an art show where I met some friends. It was winter, and we stored our coats under a bench lining the west wall. My friend introduced me to this woman who had the most vibrant mind I had come across. We hit it off right away. As the show came to a close, a man walked past me with a coat on that resembled mine. Wait, it was mine. I kindly asked him to remove the coat and give it back to me. He replied, "But it looks better on me than you." I had to hand it to him, he might've been right, but come on, man! Still, he did not hinder my mood of meeting that vibrant mind.

She texted me that night with her phone number, and we started spending time together.

It's possible to miss someone without feeling sad about it, right?

I've not seen this person in over a decade. People move

through our lives, and sometimes we are a major piece of their history, most of the time we are merely a footnote. Even though I am most likely a footnote to her, I'm okay with that. 'The Köln Concert' is a way to keep her alive in my mind. Sure, it's her from years ago, but those that pass through our lives also get frozen in time. Relationships that end are not failures, just bad timing. One of my greatest fears is that I forget. Forget the people who have impacted my life. I want to remember her touch and her voice and the mole on her cheek. I want to remember what it was like being with a creative and intellectual person, sitting in the same room with her as we worked on our projects, breaking to share some revelation, peeking over each other's shoulder to see what we were writing. To debate and argue, lovingly. To disagree, respectively. To make love. To laugh, my favourite thing was to zero in on what made her laugh and exploit that at every opportunity.

'The Köln Concert' has become something familiar to me, it makes me feel good and sad and angry and melancholic all at the same time. When I played for my friends, my ex-girlfriend was there. I slipped into a dream that included her wherever she is in the world. A thought popped into her head: she should turn on 'The Kohn Concert.' Something she hadn't listened to in a very long time. As she's listening, she is transported to my apartment, where I am playing the piece. The notes sync up. In my dream, it's raining, and each raindrop creates a memory for both of us, synching up our thoughts. We sit in our respective worlds, the worlds we have created for ourselves, worlds that are entirely different from when ours had collided all those years ago. We smile at each other across oceans and continents. However idealized our memories, we smile. The music creates a small space in our minds and hearts for each other.

When I finished playing, my friends were gone. It was dark outside. Chairs were empty. I get it - the piece is long. It didn't matter because there was still someone else in the room with me, and before she disappeared, she smiled at me with a slight smile. The mole on her cheek disappearing into her dimple.

Sometimes, light snacks and refreshments of the alcohol variety are not enough. Sometimes, what you need is a piece of music from decades ago.

THE CAT AND THE BEETLE

The Man and the cat made a gentleman's agreement: "Stay three meters from me at all times and we'll get along just fine." They even shook on it, hand to paw. As The Man would soon see, the cat was not reliable when it came to deals made with a hand/paw shake. Perhaps The Man should have made the cat sign an official notarized contract?

Summer in Austin, Texas, is hot. Like disgusting hot. The Man was in Austin for work, but also, he was housesitting for a friend. The plan was to take a local transit bus from the airport into the city and walk the rest of the way. If he didn't get lost, the walk should take about two hours.

Halfway through the walk, The Man regretted this course of action. The hotter he got, the heavier his backpack became. After the first hour, the heat rose into his brain, making it fuzzy. Somehow he didn't get lost, but in this world of modern transportation, he questioned many of his decisions. As usually happened with this kind of journey, the arrival helped erase the past two hours of intense and thick heat.

For the last forty-five minutes of his walk, he focused on the house key that was hidden in a flower pot along the side of the house. What if the key wasn't there? Where would he walk next? Would he just keep walking? When he arrived, there had to be twenty potted plants. He looked for the aloe plant, finally finding the key dug into the dirt of the third one.

Inside the house, The Man disabled the alarm, stood in the silence.

Being used to apartment buildings, where the neighbour's dog could be heard like it was right in the room, the man was unaccustomed to all the silence and space.

And the darkness.

If he didn't turn on the lights, he'd be in complete darkness, unlike his apartment, where visual noise flooded through windows and the cracks between the doors and the walls.

The silence.

His apartment ran parallel to train tracks, the ear becomes deaf to the noise, and the trains were only noticed in their absence. The Man took a few steps into the house, stopped, listened to the silence. Few more steps. Stopped. Listened.

He had everything he would need: food in the fridge, a job to go to every day, a car to get to that job, a roof overheard. The most important thing he had was time. When do we ever have time anymore to just be in a place where no one really knows where you are? To bring things down to a base level, root out all the garbage in our heads and attempt to make sense of your place in the world?

The Man's routine started on the first day. He got up early, practiced tai chi and meditated for ten minutes. These are things he had done in his life before, but he needed to re-incorporate them, break away the physical and emotional scar tissue that had taken over his body.

One of his goals for the week was to push through that initial period of returning to exercise, the first few days when his body cried out in opposition, only to thank him later. Having experience in training as an athlete, albeit many years ago, he understood that he needed to give his body time. Within a few days or weeks, he'd cross that threshold of pain and transition into his body craving to be active.

After almost dying in an accident and having someone close to him die, the last half year was dedicated to a lot of sitting around and waiting. Eating lots of food that came prepared and processed or delivered. Take-out containers overflowed his apartment garbage cans. He had become obsessed with existential detective shows, mostly from Britain. There was no shortage of these shows, and most of his nights consisted of eating take-out while watching a grisly murder being solved by a misanthropic depressive. He shouldn't have been drinking alcohol, but he was bored. A few beers here and there wouldn't hurt, but a few beers here and there in one night consecutively does. None of this did any good for his body or motivation.

It was all to stop: the processed food, alcohol, cigarettes. The only thing he'd keep for now is cigarettes. One cigarette, to be precise. At night, on the patio, as he reexamined his place in the world.

After tai chi and meditation, he ate breakfast and made his way to work. He put his head down and focused. Ate the lunch of an avocado sandwich and celery sticks he made at home. He was trying to be more sympathetic to his body. For this particular project, he was just there, making sure a renovation was happening on time and on schedule. He spoke with the project manager every day, every day things ran smoothly. There was nothing for him to do except sit and wait until it was time for him to return home.

At night, more exercise that usually involved solo yoga. There was a space on the second floor between the bedrooms that had a shag carpet. The air was cooler here, and he was able to breathe.

He wrote in a diary, something he hadn't done in many years. The diary was less a journal than a collection of the activities he undertook. He wanted to stay on top of things, to be more committed to something. Committed to an ideal, a belief that he could become a better person.

Later in the evening, he walked the neighbourhood. The

sun was down, and the humidity wasn't so thick. Downtown wasn't too far away, and as he walked, live music spilled out of bars, and people generally seemed to be having a great time. The poverty of America was never far away, all he had to do was slip down a side street, get off the main strip. He didn't mind the sweat or the heat as much when he knew where he was going.

Before bed, The Man sat outside on the patio, thinking and having his cigarette. The patio light was directly overhead, capturing the blue smoke in mid-air. A creek ran between his house and the neighbours. Everything was quiet at night except the creek and the occasional car that drove down the street and the crinkling of his cigarette when he took a drag.

In the morning, the cat usually let The Man know when it was feeding time. He purred his head off while keeping his three-meter distance away. The cat backed away, and The Man filled his food bowl. He drank his coffee as the cat ate.

On the second day, the cat violated the agreement. The Man was practicing yoga, and when he held the position of downward facing dog, the cat lightly stepped through the archway The Man made with his body. He had to exit the position, swatting away the cat. Every time he went back into position, the cat crept within the three-meter radius.

On the third day, while meditating in the morning, The Man felt the cat approaching. Whiskers rubbed along his bare shin. It was as though the cat was a mischievous Buddha, attempting to distract him from his practice. What The Man failed to recognize was that the cat wasn't trying to distract him. With his owners gone, he wanted affection. Wanted someone to pet him, rub under his chin, acknowledge him.

Years ago, The Man rented a room in a house. The owners got a kitten, and it terribly misbehaved. Ripping up curtains, clawing away at skin. The Man was never a cat person. After a few weeks, the kitten poked its head into his bedroom at night and soon slept on the end of his bed. The Man came to be friends with the kitten. When it came time for The Man to move out, he made the decision to ask the owners if he could bring the kitten with him, as they had no love for it. What he didn't know was on that day, they decided they had enough of the kitten and its claws. They had put it to sleep for being mischievous.

The Man never wanted to love another cat again.

On the fourth morning, The Man said goodbye to the cat. While eating his lunch, he wondered what the cat was up to at home. When he returned, he said hello and inquired about his day.

The cat joined him outside on the patio at night for his cigarette. Sometimes they both sat there watching a spider spinning its web. Sometimes The Man watched the cat chase beetles that scurried up between the floorboards of the patio. Soon, they quietly talked about a great many things.

"Why did he have to die?" The Man asked.

"Because we all die," said the cat. "It was his time."

"That's a bull shit answer," said The Man.

"It might be bull shit, but it's the truth."

The Man wasn't good with bugs, so when a beetle crawled over the top of his bare foot, he jumped, took his sandal in hand and slammed down hard on the fast moving insect. Down and down again, he lost control, violently attacking the insect. The beetle flipped on to its back, and its tentacles reached towards him. He slammed the sandal down again and again and again. He lost all sense of where he was - the house, his work, Austin. All that mattered was not only killing the beetle but obliterating it.

Returning to Austin, to the house, sweating from the exertion, the beetle squashed against the wood, The Man looked up to find the cat sitting on its rump, head peeked to the side, watching him with unblinking eyes. They stood like this for a while, until finally, The Man slumped down into his chair, tears silently running down his cheek, his left hand shielding his face from judgment.

The cat slowly walked over, rubbed his furry head around his ankles in an infinity symbol. The cat was letting the man know that it was okay, it was the beetle's time. After sitting out there for a long time, The Man went inside, returning with some paper towel to clean up the beetle carcass.

On the final night, The Man arrived home, said hello to the cat, but there was no movement in the house. Sometimes the cat wanted to be outside for the day. Out on the patio, still no sign of the cat. He leaned over the fence that ran parallel to the creek. The patio jutted out from the top of a hill, the hill quite a steep slant towards the creek. The Man looked over the railing, immediately caught the eye of the cat whose left front paw seemed to be stuck between two heavy rocks.

The Man climbed the fence, slid down the hill, stopping right beside the cat. When he tried to move the cat, it cried out in pain. The Man slowed his breathing, took the free paw in his hand, rubbed the top of its head, trying to calm it down.

The Man was brought back to the hospital room, where he held his father's hand, rubbing the top of his head as he lay unconscious. His father was sedated, but if he asked him questions, he responded with a squeeze of the hand.

"I should be doing better," said The Man.

Hand squeeze.

"I could be doing more with my life."

Hand squeeze.

It was his time to die.

It wasn't time for the cat to die.

"This is going to hurt," The Man told the cat. "But only for a moment." He lifted the rocks off the cat's paw, gently pulling it free. The cat ran away up the hill, stopped at the top to look back at The Man.

For a brief moment, he saw something other than the cat. He saw that the cat held a kind of simple truth, one that seemed to continually elude The Man. In spending so much time attempting to understand, to process, to make sense of the past, it only kept unravelling further.

One fleeting moment.

He couldn't exactly put his finger on what it was or what it meant. He decided not even to try.

The cat only meowed furiously. It was time to eat.

I KILLED SOMETHING TODAY

Last year, driving along the highway to the airport early in the morning, a truck clipped my car on the side, sending me spinning across three lanes. Someone screamed, and I realized that someone was me. The scream came from looking to my left and seeing another truck heading towards me at full speed. This second truck hit me from behind, sending me crashing into the guardrail.

A few months passed before the insurance was worked out, and I picked up a new car. Still a few more months before I could drive on highways again.

My extended family lives in another city a five-hour drive away, and there's an alternative route that largely avoids the main highways. Highways with all its trucks travelling too fast, swaying into the lanes beside them. Now that I'm somewhat back to driving on highways, there's a new addition - a truck that has an extended trailer. Essentially, it's the size of two trucks being driven by one person. How is this safe?

Enough about my anxieties around highways and trucks.

These backroads are quite pleasant to drive on, except when you get an impatient person behind, wanting to drive faster and taking unnecessary risks of passing you in oncoming lanes. I mean, there's only so fast one can drive on these curvy roads. It's my policy to never give another driver the middle finger - this doesn't help anyone, and it doesn't make me feel better. Instead, as they pass, I smile straight ahead and give them a thumb's up like I whole-heartedly agree with their current reckless behaviour. Sure, passive-aggressive, but instead of provoking anger, it just creates confusion from them. I'll take confusion over anger any day, especially when it involves another car, which is basically a death machine on wheels.

Driving along a stretch with a lake on one side and farmland on the other, I had two such drivers behind me. The road being curvy, there were no ideal opportunities to pass, and even these two drivers were not willing to take a guess at whether an oncoming car was coming around the bend or not.

That's about when the groundhog decided to try and cross the street. The groundhog popped on to the road and sprinted across the two lanes. He basically ran right into my car. I had a split-second choice: I could slam on the brakes, or I could hit him. If I slammed on the brakes, the car behind me was so close that he would surely crash into my trunk, and the car behind him would crash into his trunk.

So, I hit the groundhog, or I should say, I killed the groundhog. There's no way that he could have survived, and if he did, he'd be in bad shape. His relatives would have to decide whether or not to pull the plug. Not to get too graphic, but I felt the small body of that animal shatter on impact and, in my mirror, saw bloody parts still flying through the air, landing on the hood of the car behind me.

Kept my composure, kept driving. Stopping at the first chance and just sat there. I killed something today. I mean, I've killed mosquitoes, but nothing else of much substance. That groundhog, whose days consisted of digging, eating, sleeping, then here I come along into his territory with my big dumb metal tank and smash his body to smithereens. I didn't mean to do it. Why didn't he wait ten seconds to cross the road? He would have had a clear path.

Tired, I decided to lower my seat back and tried for some rest. I had been running on empty for a while, emotions running high, that kind of thing. What I needed the least at the moment was to get into another car accident, something that flashed in front of my eyes at least once every time I got behind the wheel. In that flash, I was back in my car a few months ago, spinning, screaming, watching a truck heading right towards me, and I knew without a doubt that I was going to die. Did that groundhog know he was going to die when he woke up in the morning?

After my nap, I kept heading towards my destination. Along the way, I stopped to caffeinate myself. When it came time to order, the person behind the cash smiled a knowing smile and said, "Hey, haven't seen you in a while, where've you been?" It was a small city, one that I had never been to in all the times I drove to Ottawa. So, to the best of my knowledge, I'd never set foot in this coffee shop.

She picked up on my confusion and said, "The usual?" I nodded slowly, still partially confused but also curious as to what my usual would be somewhere I've never been. She wrote my name on the cup without asking. I moved over to where the barista was preparing my usual, smiled at me in a similar style as the cashier and said, "Some room at the top, soy, right?" I blinked three times and nodded. She handed me the drink and said, "Nice to see you back!" The cup was hot in my hand, but I didn't feel it. I lifted the drink for the name written on the side: Jeffrey. Assuming that they had mistaken me for someone else, I couldn't help but think about two truths: 1. My first name is actually Jeffrey; 2. I do like room and soy.

Now, these experiences really happened on the same trip. I really did kill a groundhog, and there was an alleged mistaken identity at a coffee shop. This is the moment where I would take this down a strange tangent, creating some kind of alter ego named Jeffrey Buchanan (my real first name and the street I grew up on), who is a secret agent

35

that takes his downtime in small-town Ontario. I had been somewhere in rural Russia, infiltrating a small-arms factory that was making deals counter to international sanctions. After the barista recognized me at the local coffee shop, it would be time for me to move on because I need to live an anonymous life of solitude.

But I just don't have the energy for this right now.

All I wanted to do was get to my destination. Actually, I just returned from visiting my family the previous day. A frantic phone call came from my mother in the evening, "They've moved him to the hospice, I think you should come back."

Making my way through the small town and returning to the backroads, I thought again of that groundhog. How would his family know he died? No groundhog police force makes the visit or call to their hole and let them know their father/brother/husband died.

An hour later, I had to eat. I hadn't since the previous day. If I was to actually make it, I needed to eat. I pulled into a rest stop and loaded up on the worst meal I ever had: two hamburgers, poutine, chicken nuggets. Inhaling the food, someone said, "Um, Paul, right?" I looked up to find an old man squinting his eyes at all my food. "That's quite a spread, huh?" How in the hell, on the way to a destination where I've never ever met anyone else I know, at a rest stop somewhere between nowhere and never been, do I run into someone I used to work with years ago?

And he wanted to talk. We caught up on the place we used to work and what we're doing now. He and his brother were on a weekend fishing trip, got a flat tire and were waiting for help. Limiting my answers to 'um, sure' or 'yeah' or 'right,' he still didn't get the point. Finally, he went away.

But he wasn't finished yet!

Slamming the rest of the hamburgers, nuggets and fries into my face, I went to throw away my garbage and there he was, seemingly waiting for me. He wanted to introduce me to his brother.

Why can't we be honest with each other? What I really wanted to say was that I'm in the middle of a race, and it is quite literally life and death. Yes, I have time to sit down and eat a ridiculously unhealthy meal, but I needed fuel. Yes, I was pleasant to you earlier, but now you are taking up time on my clock. If I am being rude to you, would you rather me tell you that my father has been ill the past couple of years and the last time I saw him I said I needed to take a work trip and would come back right after? I think he understood me. But then my mother called to say the doctor sedated him and he is unconscious but in no pain. Should I tell you that he could die at any point and me standing here talking to someone I knew years ago and hadn't thought about since then is something I don't want to be doing at this point? Good day to you then, sirs, and let me be on my way.

Instead, I went with a few more 'yeahs' and 'sure' and finally got the hell out of there.

This being Canada, it started snowing around the time I had an hour left of driving. This was April. It happens.

For this last hour, I was to be on a two-lane highway, which, as the blizzard intensified, became one lane. Passed cars in ditches as the snow piled up and came down faster. Up here in Canada, we have summer and winter tires, which until this moment, I thought was a racket. The week previous, it being April, I switched to my summer tires. So, whenever I even thought about touching the brake, the car started swerving on the fresh snow.

Still, people drove fast, passing into the snow-covered

second lane just to get a little ahead. And then it came: the truck. Barreling down the highway behind me at full speed. It approached fast, slipped into the ankle-high snow of the left-hand lane and started to pass me.

This was it - this time, the truck would get me. I was in a race to get to the hospice before my dad died. I didn't want him to die alone, but really, he wouldn't be alone. My mother was there as always. No, I was the one that didn't want to hear of his death while I was alone, and by extension, I didn't want to die alone here on this highway by this truck.

Now, I'll get run off the road by this truck that will reach his destination five minutes sooner, and as the snow piles up on my car, I'll get the call. Or worse, my mother will have to deal with the death of her husband and son.

I braced myself for when the truck blew past, kicking up so much snow that I couldn't see out the windshield. Knuckles white, I kept my foot off the brake and the steering wheel straight. Before I knew it, he was off in the distance in front of me, and I was alive.

Hours later, I arrived at my destination and spent the next three days and nights at the hospice.

PART TWO: IDENTITY

MARRIED WITH CHILDREN

Early Sunday morning, I pulled myself out of bed and drove to the badlands. Okay, not the badlands, just the suburbs. My destination: a McDonald's. Who *wouldn't* want to hang out on a Sunday morning at a McDonald's in the suburbs?

Sitting inside the McDonald's, there were three older men at another table, hands around coffee cups, staring at me. This was their McDonald's. They probably knew most of the people who frequented the establishment. I was definitely in enemy territory. And they knew it.

I took the top off my coffee and set it down on the table. If they tried anything, my plan was to thrust the burning hot coffee into one guy's face and kick the other two in the knees and the balls, respectively.

Whenever I entered a room, I scanned for escape routes or possible dangers. I didn't know where this came from, and at this point in my life, it was automatic. I didn't always consciously know the most efficient and direct way to escape in any given situation, it now just came intuitively. However, if you were to ask me the fastest way to escape from that particular McDonald's, it would have been to take one of the chairs at my table, throw it at the large window behind me and hop out. This way, you avoided having to shove people aside. In a crisis, people slowed you down.

Anyways.

I wanted to have music in my life and found a used keyboard for sale online. The catch was having to drive all the way out to the badlands and meet the seller in the McDonald's. This McDonald's, the one I was currently sitting in, having a staring competition with three elderly men.

Ten minutes after the seller was supposed to be there, I emailed to let her know that I was sitting inside. As I received her email saying her husband was coming to meet me, a middle-aged man stepped in - also someone that didn't belong here. The three older men stopped, switched from staring at me to him. He pointed at me, I nodded my head, we shook hands, and he said the keyboard was outside in his car. Walking by the three older men, I waved goodbye. Their balls were safe for the moment.

We walked to his BMW, and he took the keyboard out of the backseat and showed it to me. "I brought some batteries," he said. "Do you want to test it out?" I flipped the keyboard in my hands, and he loaded it up with some batteries. "Works fine, see," he said, as he banged on some of the keys, which I agreed all seemed to be functioning. He popped the batteries back out. I mean, why not throw in the batteries? Cheap.

Calling this man cheap was judgmental. Something I've come to accept about myself over the years is that I am judgmental. It's fun, try it before you knock it. It comes from having a rich internal life. Patterns are created in my head - the way people are supposed to act and how society is supposed to function - and when actions deviate from these patterns, the judgment gene kicks in.

"Hey," he said. "There's also a learning book that goes along with it." He reached back into the car, pulled out a book that had a hand-drawn girl sitting at a piano. Why would I need this?

Oh, crap.

On the way over to my car, he asked, "So, you're buying this for your kid?"

Right.

I had two choices at this point. 1. I could have been honest and told him that it was for me. For some reason, I felt strange to admit that a grown adult man was buying a keyboard like I should be ashamed of this or something; or 2. I could lie. Just agree with him and hopefully end the conversation there. But this guy was a real Chatty Cathy except his name was Neil.

Before I even properly reviewed and processed my two options, I blurted out, "Yeah, it's for my kid." The main problem with going with #2 was follow-up questions.

"How old is your kid?" He asked.

Damn.

"Ten years old," I replied. "He wanted to learn the piano, but I figured, why not get a keyboard first cause he'll probably lose interest. Kids these days, huh?"

"You don't have to tell me," he said. "My daughter hardly even touched that keyboard. What's your son's name?"

"James," I said. James is a strong name.

Okay, so within 30 seconds, I'd gone from a single guy living downtown to a suburban dad with a 10-year-old son named James, who really wanted to play the piano. A lot could happen in the time it took to walk across a parking lot.

"So, the wife sent you all the way out here on a Sunday morning?" He asked.

I decided to have some fun, because, after that loaded statement, why not?

"Ex-wife," I said.

I mean, my wife? That's kind of presumptuous. Maybe we're not married? Maybe we're common law? Maybe I never wanted to be married in the first place? Maybe my wife cheated on me with my best friend, and I caught them one night in our bed - OUR BED! - after returning home late from work? Maybe I'm married to a man? Because it's 2018.

Also, because I have no son named James, and I've never been married or divorced or am not even currently in a relationship of any kind or even really lived with a partner for any length of time.

When he assumed I had kids, I could have explained to him that no, I did not have any, that this keyboard was for me, that I learned piano as a kid, tried to teach myself guitar, but my guitar attacked me, and that I want music in my life. And I don't need your stupid learning book.

People make this assumption all the time. The world is made for conscious coupling. Eating in restaurants alone is out. A married person once asked me, "How do you eat?" Going to movies or to the theatre? You're always at fault for making the seating arrangements uneven. There is no one sharing my mortgage or other bills, there is no 'single person' rate.

Last year, I was staying in a Bed and Breakfast in Austin, Texas. For three mornings, it was just me and Nick, the proprietor of the business. We had great conversations about local music and film scenes. On my last morning, a couple around my age entered the breakfast area, and Nick offered a hearty 'Happy Birthday!' to the woman. They both paused when they saw me and awkwardly joined me at the other end of the long table. We sat there in silence, and because I can read minds, they thought the same thing as me: *What's with this weirdo guy sitting alone ruining this special birthday breakfast that had been planned?* Because Bed and Breakfasts are also not for single people.

"It's for James' birthday," I said as I snatched the keyboard from him, got in my car and screeched out of that lonely McDonald's parking lot.

On my long drive back downtown from the badlands, I thought about my son James. Thought about how my life might've been with just a few different decisions. I couldn't even imagine who would be the mother of my child. No one from my past. The good thing about a relationship ending is that you have the choice to keep going as friends or never see that person again. With a child, you're tied to that person forever. Everyone tells me that I'll want kids when I meet the right person. I'm getting to the point where I'll be Old Dad, which means people meeting us for the first time will always mistake me for his grandfather.

Let's just say I meet the right person. We have a kid, we name him James. Now what? I'm good with kids, I've done some teaching. I talk to them like they're adults. But I only dealt with them for thirty minutes at a time, and I gave them back. I can't give James back to anyone. He grows up, maybe resents me in his teenage years and through his twenties. I wanted to be the Cool Dad, but I am definitely not cool. I'm just Old Dad. We reconcile as he gets older, he has a family of his own and then I slowly fade away into old age.

So, next time, I'll go with #1.

However, I was in the Dollar Store not too long ago buying some ridiculous Halloween items for a party. The nice woman at the checkout looked at the assorted items, looked at me, raised her eyebrows. I smiled and said, "It's for my son James, he's really into Halloween." It was June. She just shrugged her shoulders at the unnecessary information.

Perhaps I could use my imaginary son James for when I'm doing some of the ridiculous stuff I do? Instead of people judging me for it, I can pin it on him. They can judge James.

~

After my car accident, I had to answer the same three questions multiple times: "Are you married? Do you have any dependents? Do you live alone?"

Let's set aside, for now, the inherent judgments embedded in each of these questions. Remember: I am a highly judgmental person, so somewhat understand the logic in these questions. The short answers are: No, no and yes.

The tow truck driver, who had mysteriously appeared before the police and the ambulance, suggested we sat in his truck to get out of the cold. We sat quietly for a few minutes until he wanted to make small talk, starting with, "Are you married?" When I answered no, he shrugged and said, "That's probably for the best." Although he was trying to be kind, it was along the lines of 'Who needs the old ball and chain, right?' kind of thing. I was still in somewhat of a state of shock and didn't have the energy to engage him in conversation about it.

On the phone with the insurance company, the representative inquired about whether I was married or had any dependents. I was beginning to think maybe I was married, or at least, people were trying to give me some hints about my major life decisions.

Waiting to see a doctor, I felt myself sinking further and further into exhaustion and pain. She arrived, and the first three questions were: "Are you married? Do you have any dependents? Do you live alone?" The living alone question was important because I had a concussion and needed to be woken up every few hours, or I might not wake up at all. But the other questions confused me. Should I be married? I understand this is a thing that people do, but it never seemed to be in the cards for me. Perhaps I should just find someone willing enough to put up with my poor attitude and buy a ring and walk down that aisle?

For the next few days, I watched a lot of television. I almost watched the entire first two seasons of *Bojack Horseman* in one sitting. I pulled myself together and went back to the doctor's office for my first physiotherapy appointment. She had to re-assess me, and the first question she asked was: "Are you married?" I paused. Maybe it was the amount of television I watched, or my complete lack of any strength to try and explain that yes, the institution of marriage is still going strong even though culturally it is outdated and antiquated, some people are not really avoiding it out of any protest - we just can't find a partner to love and who will love us. Some of us just aren't lucky enough.

So, instead, I just said: "Yes, I'm married."

"Oh, really?" The physiotherapist said. "What's your wife's name?"

I also didn't have the energy to bring up the fact that it's probably not wise to gender marriage. Marriage might be outdated, but as I already mentioned, it's 2018; we can all get married now, and one shouldn't make assumptions.

Instead, I just said: "Diane." Diane is a character in *Bojack Horseman*. For the past few days, my brain had been foggy, but at that moment, something cleared. I saw her clearly. I saw my wife, Diane.

"Diane is a nice name," the physiotherapist said.

"Yes, Diane has helped me so much. She's incredibly smart, much smarter than me. We really make each other better."

I don't know what came over me, and I provided way too much information about my wife, Diane. The physiotherapist was probably sorry that she asked.

"Diane and I met when we were finishing university. I had started working, and she was taking a Master's Degree. She'd go on to do a Ph.D. in international relations. Like I said, much smarter than me. We are quite the match. We

49

both work from home, but it's okay, we like being around each other. We can work quietly in the same space, but also, we like bouncing ideas off each other. We're a team! She's creative also, like really creative. Naturally creative. An amazing writer and although we are a romantic partnership, we have independent lives. We do almost everything together, but we have separate interests, which we both regard as a healthy addition to our already amazing relationship. We're really perfect for each other. Maybe at my next appointment, Diane can come, and you can meet her? I think the two of you would really hit it off. We've talked about having kids. James for a boy. Jane for a girl."

The physiotherapist had gone silent, but not a good kind of silence. I took my cue to shut up about Diane, and we continued on with the assessment. I had become one of those people, the kind who insisted on projecting to the world just how happy they are in their relationship. In reality, in-between the jovial social media pictures and constant insistence about HOW MUCH MORE HAPPIER WE ARE THEN YOU, it's just another sad and failed relationship experiment. Or, in my case, a non-existent failed relationship.

But I liked the sound of this Diane, she had characteristics of a person I'd really like to be around.

I was so convincing that I went home thinking Diane would be there waiting for me. But when I opened my front door, the place was empty because I'm not married, I have no dependents, and I live alone.

TAXI DRIVER

Outside a discount grocery store, I stood freezing my ass off. I was heading to the west end of the city, not west end downtown, farther than that, much farther. Past where the streetcars stopped running.

I had a meeting scheduled, one of those kinds of meetings that you wonder why you agreed to it and right up to when it happens, you're trying to get out of it. My plan was to hop on a streetcar, ride it directly to the end of the line and jump in a taxi from there. The end of the line was in the middle of nowhere with not a cab in sight. And exactly what everyone else in the world thought Canada was like all the time - one of those days so cold, where you barely kept it together outside.

With the grocery store as my North Star, I headed towards it, the idea being I could pretend to be shopping for groceries while I called for a cab. Inside, I arranged for a taxi and kept watch loitering around the legumes.

A taxi came speeding down the entrance and stopped right in front of the grocery store. I ran outside, and the driver put down the passenger side window and asked, "Are you, Carl?" Now, every once in a while, we are fortunate to be present in a specific moment in time, a moment where our life could change, could continue on our usual trajectory or go off in an unknown direction. I thought about the meeting I was trying to get to and how much I didn't want to go. Added to this, the ridiculously cold weather. Plus, there was only so much loitering I could do before having to buy something. So, I made a decision. He asked again, "Are you, Carl?" And I said, "Yes."

From the backseat, I watched the driver plugin some

coordinates into his GPS, and we were off. Somewhere at the grocery store was someone named Carl waiting for a taxi. My bones were frigid, about ready to crack. Besides, he could take my taxi when it got there.

I didn't know where we were going, and I didn't care. At that moment, in that taxi, I was Carl.

We reached our destination of what looked like a conference centre, and a woman came running towards the car. She thrust the door open and asked desperately, "Are you, Carl?" I nodded, she paid for my taxi and ushered me inside. "They are all ready and waiting for you." When we got inside, she slapped one of those 'Hello My Name Is...' name tags on my chest. Carl was printed in black sharpie.

Those moments I spoke of earlier come every once in a while, but here I already had another chance. As I walked into that packed conference centre, I thought about Carl. Usually, I am plagued by anxiety, bouts of depression and have a list of insecurities a mile long. In social situations, especially networking-type events, I can be awkward and often the weird guy standing off in the corner.

Not Carl.

Carl was confident, he was charming and charismatic. He knew how to handle a crowd and had no problem being appropriately personal. People knew when Carl entered a room and when he left, they talked about him. Carl's a man that got noticed.

On my way up to the stage, at least ten people stopped to introduce themselves to me. Men, at least ten years my senior, slapped me on the back. My head was high, and I felt for one of the first times in my life what it was like to be comfortable with yourself. As the woman who first met me went up on stage to introduce me, I suddenly realized that I was the keynote speaker for whatever this conference was about. But I wasn't scared because Carl didn't get scared. Carl ate fear for breakfast.

The conference was a gathering of people in all forms of media. Well, it just so happened that I was very familiar with this subject. She introduced me to a roar of applause, and I stepped up to the microphone.

You should have heard the dramatic pause I took. I let the air be sucked out of the room, but not out of fear or nervousness, out of anticipation of the profound talk that was about to happen. I can't exactly remember everything I said, but I spoke about the positive parts of our business, the growth and the exciting new opportunities coming our way. I also talked about how we could get better, that we had a long road ahead of us, but together we could achieve success. By the end of that speech, I had the crowd in the palm of my hands. They were cheering and clapping as I stepped off the stage. It's not about what you said, but how you said it.

The real Carl popped into my head. I wondered if he waited in front of that grocery store, and a taxi pulled up, and the driver asked, "Are you, Paul?" And Carl, being cold and impatient, took the taxi and stepped into my life. Maybe he had that same kind of moment, but for him, he got my anxieties and insecurities. And just as I thought this was a fair trade-off, as my adoring public was shaking hands with me, I walked from the stage and saw him enter the conference room. The woman that introduced me was talking to him and pointing at me. She knew that he was the real Carl, and the three of us shared an intimate moment of confusion/recognition in that crowded room.

I felt my head lower, my shoulders went round, and I couldn't look anyone in the eyes. I slipped through my cheering and adoring public, out a side door and back into the cold. I called for a taxi, and when he showed up, he put down the passenger side window and asked, "Are you, Paul?" To which I replied, somewhat defeated, "Yes."

This new taxi was one of those van taxi's, which made it all the sadder, getting an entire van to myself. Where should I sit? Window or aisle? The side door slid open, and I jumped inside. It was getting late, I just wanted to get home. I grumbled the intersection of my place, but we still weren't going anywhere.

Carl wouldn't have put up with this. But I'm not Carl.

"Is there a problem?" I asked.

The driver fiddled with his phone and finally turned and handed it to me.

"Here," he said. "Put in the address, and we'll find it."

Wasn't it his job to know where we're going? He had a phone that was unknown to me, and I couldn't figure it out. I crawled into the front passenger seat and said, "Just drive, I'll show you where to go."

"I'm sorry," he said. "I just moved here, and this is my first night on the job. Ask me to go anywhere in Ottawa, and I could take you there. Toronto? This city is a maze."

"It's not so bad, really," I said. "It's more of a grid, and if you figure out north and south and east and west, you'll get it."

I told him I'm from Ottawa, and he knew the exact intersection of my childhood home. He told me he was going to business school during the day, driving at night. Toronto was intimidating him a little. We reached my place, I paid and got out. Through the windshield, I watched him as he fiddled some more with his phone, trying to figure out his next destination. I walked back, opened the passenger side door.

"This is a strange suggestion, but would you be interested

in me driving around with you for the night and helping you get around?"

The driver's shoulders dropped with relief, and he nodded furiously.

Our first stop was Bloor and Christie. "Okay," I said. "Up Shaw, east on Dundas, then north. It's one way up to Bloor, so we have to double back."

On the way, I told him how I used to live in an apartment near Christie Pits Park. It was above a bar, and one night we heard a loud crash. Someone had been thrown through the front window of the bar and lay on the sidewalk covered in broken glass. The thrower (we assumed) jumped through the shattered window and started punching the guy in the face. The bartender yelled, "The police are on the way."

We dropped off our passengers at Davenport and Ossington. I took the driver on a little trip east to an office building that I spent many years working in. They used to construct Model T's in this building until it changed hands and became a peanut factory. I learned just about every fundamental element of storytelling in that building.

Two young men flagged us down, and we drove all the way to Dufferin and College. If you could believe it, they walked right into another apartment that I lived in. This was where I fell in love for the first time, solidified a friendship that became one of the most important relationships of my life.

We got a call for a pickup on Roncesvalles, near High Park. Go west, they said. And we did. After our pick up, I told the taxi driver about when I lived down the street. It was here where I fell in love for the second time, actually when I thought about it, it was the last time I fell in love. There had been people since, but nothing like that feeling at that time. I told him about how I was fiddling around in my apartment the other day, and it dawned on me - on that particular date,

I marked a different kind of anniversary, the anniversary of when that relationship ended four years ago. Four years. That was about 1460 days, and nothing since then had been as good, as real, as deep. It wasn't even her anymore, she had faded from my memory and been somewhat idealized in my head. It felt genuine at the time. I remember elements of it being real.

I guess I had just been lonely, my small apartment seemed so empty, especially when I thought of 1460 days of being single. That's a lot of days. I had music or a podcast playing in the background at all times, even when I was reading. I couldn't bear how silent it was, my thoughts spiralled down too far, too quickly.

I directed the taxi driver up to Dufferin and Lawrence. When I lived up here, I went into a self-imposed exile. Removed myself from everything, learned how to be alone, learned how to be away from people. Isolated myself from others, from me. In some ways, even though I got myself out of it, got back to the world of people and friends and family, I never fully brought down those walls.

As the sun rose over the horizon, and his shift was ending, we drove in silence south to my place. Sitting in the idling van, I went over with him some last-minute ideas of how I eventually navigated my way through the city. The CN Tower is south, the 401 is north. The rest was easy, the rest could be figured out. What couldn't be figured out was what happened on those streets, in those houses, behind closed doors.

Being a person is messy. Sometimes I forgot about all the details of what happened across all those homes. I got sad sometimes, thinking of how I might have missed out on things, made the wrong decisions.

Regrets!

Time travel.

Not live in the past, but revel in the people that have come and gone, what they've given me, what perhaps I had given them.

The things I had seen!

Not everything was good, not everything was to my taste, but when I had been able to be open, truly be open, opened my heart and my mind and my eyes, to be inside a moment and to truly be awake in that moment, even those split decisions that changed everything, that changed the trajectory of my life in a way that might not seem reasonable at first, but only at first, because with time perhaps that decision changed everything and led me to places that I couldn't imagine, that I had no projection of in my mind's eye or my imagination or could have possibly been caught in that space right between my eyes and eyebrows.

These places we ventured to tonight, these weren't just places to sleep or to eat. They were places where I fell in love, cried my heart out, laughed my ass off, shared moments with others that were lodged in my brain, forgotten and only remembered when I saw the front doors of houses I used to live, front porches and backyards, windows I could look through from the outside and peek in and see the ghosts of the people I lived with and see spirits that looked like me.

I waved to the taxi driver as he pulled away. He'd be okay, he'd figure out how to navigate this city with all its ghosts lurking behind closed doors.

Me? That's another story.

THE FATE OF THINGS

I'm not dying, at least of anything I am aware of. But, if you think about it, aren't we all on the journey towards death the moment we are born? Never mind, I'm not here to be a smart ass, I just read an article in the New York Times called *The Lonely Death of George Bell*. It's about what happens to someone when they die who have no dependents or next of kin. George Bell died alone in his apartment and wasn't found for at least a week when a neighbour noticed the smell.

The article was right up my alley because dying alone is something I think about pretty much every day. You could even call it a hobby. Haven't you ever played the game of — *How am I going to die?* I do it all the time. You know, for fun.

The way I might die that I think of the most is similar to George Bell. My condo is a two-storey loft with a pretty steep staircase. During one especially serious day of cleaning, I used Pledge on the wooden stairs, which made them really shiny, but also, very slippery. I figured this was it. This was how I was going to die. Maybe I'd wake up early one morning still half asleep and forget about the Pledge. The steps go straight down and weave around to the first floor. I'd probably break my neck as I rolled down, changing direction to slam on to the cement floor. Or, fall with such force that I'd smash right through the window where the stairs curve and bounce off the balcony.

My point is not to be morbid. We are just so scared of talking about death, which to me, is the morbid part. I've experienced death in my lifetime, and it was sad and traumatic. It really sucked. It may seem that I am making light of it, and maybe I am, but what else should we do with it? Death is something that all of us will experience, either through our friends, family, and loved ones and of course, eventually, sooner or later, ourselves. You could say it levels the playing field.

My latest favourite way of dying is by stepping out of a streetcar and getting hit by a car. If you live in Toronto, you can skip to the next paragraph. We still have streetcars in Toronto. Most streets are two lanes, so when a streetcar stops, there is still a lane between it and the sidewalk. Cars are supposed to stop to allow the streetcar passengers a safe crossing on to the sidewalk.

Strictly, in my opinion, 87% of all drivers are pretty dumb. Even though the streetcar doors open with stop signs on them and there are flashing lights, drivers speed past the open doors all the time. And more often than not, when the streetcar driver lays on the horn to let the car know they are being dumb, they usually look confused and oblivious to the fact that they could have almost killed about ten people. Whenever I exit a streetcar, I let the doors open, and I stick my head out to check and ensure that the cars have stopped. And there still has been one or two close calls.

Another game I like to play, say on a rainy Sunday when you don't feel like going anywhere is — *If I died right now, and there was an investigation into my death, what kind of profile would they come up with by going through my things?* They would definitely determine, pretty much right away, that I had been single, and for a long time. I mean, they might've already gleaned that since most likely I died by falling down the stairs. They'd think that I was pretty clean, or at least I'd hope they thought I was pretty clean. That everything had a place, and not only a place but The Right Place.

I don't really have many possessions or items that hold that much significance to me. I don't really believe in things representing people or memories or experiences. Those people or memories or experiences are a part of me, whether I have a trinket that reminds me of it or not. In fact, I recently got rid of at least half of my possessions. I live in a small condo, and one of the things I enjoy most about it is the lack of storage space. It means I can't really keep things. I spent a weekend a few weeks ago gleefully bringing box after box to the garbage bin area of the building. And to this day, I sometimes walk around my apartment, stop with my hands on hips at the well-organized closet or open the near-empty kitchen cabinets, and marvel at all the space.

One of the only things that concerned me about throwing out was my old notebooks. Two boxes of old notebooks going back twenty years. I had just automatically kept them, thinking they held something important between the covers. That they might reveal something when I'm old and (maybe, but unlikely) dying of old age. Something meaningful. Or, my kids or nephews might be interested in who I was after the streetcar accident. But really, I'm 91% sure that I'm not going to have any kids, and the family members that were dead and gone long before I got here were probably much more interesting to me because of the mystery. Besides, I'd be lying if I said there was anything profound in my notebooks. Sure, I carry one around with me everywhere, but they're mostly full of lists of things to do, or the scribbles of what probably looks like a madman to anyone else except me. There was a little tinge of regret right after I dumped the notebooks, but that has since gone away.

George Bell was a hoarder. What's the opposite of a hoarder? I actually looked it up, and don't worry, I'm not at all surprised to see that it is a form of obsessive-compulsive disorder. According to The Atlantic: "Compulsive decluttering is a pattern of behaviour that is characterized by an excessive desire to discard objects in one's home. It is sometimes called obsessive-compulsive spartanism. It is the act of throwing items, or clutter, away, or getting rid of them in an attempt to clean up what one may think is cluttered." I wrote the paragraphs about throwing stuff away and thought I should look up if there is something official that is the opposite of hoarding. This is one of the fun things about writing — when you reveal something about yourself and end up getting diagnosed with a new mental health disorder.

It fits though, because for me it's all about control. Even if I'm throwing things away, I like the power of knowing where they're going. That if I died today, right now, I'd know the fate of things.

Giving or throwing away these things created complicated feelings. There was an immediate relief, a liberation from these things that were only meaningful because I gave them meaning. Right after the liberating feelings, there was an immediate pang of regret as though I was doing something wrong or irresponsible. Shouldn't I value these things more? Feel the privilege of being able to own things? But, that's all they were: things. They are not another person smiling at me, or a tight embrace from a friend. They are not a piece of theatre unfolding in front of me. And they do nothing but remind me of all the tiny shards that have made me, instead of the person that sits here right now.

So, I've gotten rid of most of the evidence. I don't think the investigators would really gather that much information from my place. I don't leave many clues behind. I actually like to operate in the world as though I was never there. I don't really know why. For example, if I stay at a friend's house or even my mom's house, when I leave, I clean up the room in an attempt to put it back to the exact way it was before my arrival. Sure, this is a polite thing to do. What about a hotel room? I don't like cleaning staff coming into my room while I'm staying there, so I usually have the 'Do Not Disturb' sign out front. I can handle it, thank you very much. And when I leave, I make the bed and put everything back exactly how I found it. Is that weird? Probably.

A part of me believes this is sad, as though I am trying to erase my footprints behind me as I walk forward. Like a ghost. Like I was never there. In the movie *Heat*, Robert DeNiro's bank-robbing character said: "Don't let yourself get attached to anything you are not willing to walk out on in 30 seconds flat if you feel the heat around the corner." DeNiro's apartment in this movie had no furniture, so he was definitely a compulsive declutterer. But also, he might have to go on the run because he's a bank robber and murderer. I've not robbed any banks or killed anyone. I don't know what my version would be of the heat around the corner. Sometimes I just feel like I don't deserve to be in certain spaces, I don't want to take up people's time.

In addition to the game of how am I going to die, it sometimes takes me over in an even more immediate way. Another thing that I gave away was my car. It was mostly sitting unused in the parking garage of my condo building. After moving back downtown a few years ago, I just didn't need it anymore. Sometimes when I'd be driving, I'd see stupid things people do, risks they took while driving (remember 87% of all drivers are dumb), and I'd see the alternative results of their stupidity stretch out in my imagination. A driver waiting to make a left turn thinks he can make it before I get to the intersection, but of course, he cannot. Bang, five-car pile-up. I also think of this when I'm biking, which is a much more vulnerable place to be. These are just fleeting thoughts, and I'm sure I have them much more frequently than I can even recall. Just, you know, maneuvering around a giant pothole and having the vision of what could have happened.

You would think that living a life where you constantly saw all the alternatives would be debilitating and make me completely indecisive. It's actually the opposite and makes making decisions and sticking to them easy. When you're faced with a myriad of options, you pick one. It may not be the best one, it may not be the right one. But it really doesn't matter because whatever decision you make is the only one you'll see play out.

When I think about this stuff, I do take comfort in believing that we exist on a continuum. Our parents, or if your parents sucked, the people who helped you grow into the old person you've become. That there are people who have affected our lives, we've carried their lessons or burdens forward through us, and if we're lucky, pass them on to other people. Or actively break the patterns of bad stuff.

More so than actually dying, I think that's what really scares me, that I have not used the things that have been given to me by others, add to them, do something new with them. I choose to not give these things I've thrown away a second thought and instead see the details of the world around me and to pay attention to the signs and to not be afraid of what will happen. Instead, take great comfort in being here and being able to make fun of how it's all going to end.

BOOKMARKS

Sometimes when I'm at a friend's house and looking at their bookshelf, I really want to put the books in alphabetical order. How in the hell can you sleep at night with McCarthy on the top shelf and Chabon on the bottom?

A few years ago, my parents were visiting, and I had to go to work. I had not been living alone very long but had gotten used to having my own space without anyone interfering. I have not had a television for a long time - don't worry, I'm not being an asshole and smugly saying this, it's just a matter of fact - and I was nervous that my parents would get bored, leading them to snoop. I really should have hidden the condoms somewhere besides the obvious place in the top drawer of the nightstand.

After providing strict instructions as to what and what not they were to do, I left. Upon my return, I stepped in the door and with just a glance, I pointed at the bookshelf right inside the foyer and said, "What is going on over here?"

"I organized your books," my dad said.

I looked at what he did, and it was a horror show. I still can't believe it. He re-organized the books by SIZE, as in, all the hardcovers together, paperbacks, and so on.

The correct way to organize books on a shelf is alphabetically by the last name of the author, obviously. If there is more then one book by an author, they are sub-categorized by publishing date. Everyone knows this.

"But this looks better," my dad reasoned. "It's more aesthetically pleasing."

"What if I'm trying to find a Murakami book? Not the latest one, but from a few years ago? How would I find it?"

"It'll still be on your shelf, and it's not like this is an entire library."

My dad missed the point. Sure, I'm not talking about having rooms of books, and yes, it's sporadic - if ever - that I need to look up something in a mid-career Murakami book. Again, that's not the point. The point is that I should be able to organize the books on my shelf in whatever way I want to.

Organized by SIZE.

More aesthetically pleasing.

Anyway.

Perhaps it is becoming an adult, my fascination with the library or due to the invention of the ebook, my collection was getting really outdated.

First, I had moved all those books several times. I actually don't have a lot of stuff, mostly due to a lack of storage space, but most of my moving boxes were heavy. Yes, I actually did read that copy of *Ulysses*. No, I didn't understand what the hell it was all about. Did I really need to keep it on my shelf just to make myself look smart? Besides, how many people come over, see *Ulysses* and think, "Paul must really be smart." They're probably thinking, "That Paul really knows how to waste a lot of time." What about the entire shelf of circus books? Research for a failed screenplay, I swear. The screenplay was a 200-page script about an old-style circus but in contemporary times. I really got into the dark side of the circus. To this day, I can't figure out why no one wanted to produce it. *The DaVinci Code* might have been a gift, but why did I keep it and move it three different times?

Second, I am fortunate enough to live in a city that has one of the most incredibly complex and impressive library systems in the world. People that live here are pretty smug about their libraries. We're proud of them. Going to the library is cool. I pumped the breaks on my usage of the library when I was spending more time managing my holds then actually reading.

Third, since I'm a writer, I should be promoting the physical book as essential to the survival of our society. Opposite to my smugness over not owning a television, I was very pretentious when it came to ebooks. Not me, nope, a book wasn't a book unless it came in book form. After a while, when I realized I could carry around as many books as possible in my phone, the smugness was abandoned like any other numerous and ridiculous young adult pronouncements. Who cares? The words and the story are the important part. A book is a book. Get over it.

As mentioned, where I'm living now and hopefully going to stay for a long time until I can't climb the stairs anymore, has little storage. This didn't stop me from still insisting that I have two bookcases. See, this is a critical difference between living by yourself and with someone else: bad choices. A partner would have said, "We have no room, at least one of these bookcases needs to go." Maybe not bad choices, just the delay of reaching the right decision on your own.

One of the shelves needed to go. I simply needed the space. I wanted the books to go to people that would appreciate them. There is a used bookstore that buys books. Whenever I've gone there, the proprietor investigates each book, usually scoffs at the author and offers you pennies, only to resell at a highly marked up price. He's not scoffing when he's making seven dollars on that hardcover of *The Girl with the Dragon Tattoo*. I decided to have a party and invite some literary-minded friends over to take whatever they wanted. Maybe it was just a way to bribe people to visit me? Probably. I pulled the books I didn't want, and the rest were negotiable. You never know, I still might need that 1934 memoir of a circus clown.

The party was a huge success, and I did get rid of one entire bookshelf. I don't put this down to having many friends or even an interesting book collection, more that people like free stuff.

A friend of mine started working in the film and television industry, and I gave her the film books that I thought would be helpful to her. A few days later, she messaged me about a book, or more specifically, what she found inside one. She wrote, "Who is Jess?" and included a photograph of a bookmark she found in one of the film books.

Written on the bookmark was the name 'Jess' along with a phone number labelled "555-5555 @ work". I couldn't for the life of me remember anyone named Jess. The name and number were found in a book on Francis Ford Coppola. Okay, so I was obsessed with Coppola around the time *Apocalypse Now* was re-released. I discovered, as most aspiring filmmakers do, the documentary *Hearts of Darkness*, about the making of the movie. I watched the *Godfather* movies way too many times, even the third one, which I believe to be highly underrated. All the crappy films too, and he's made his fair share. Maybe ten years ago? What was I doing ten years ago?

I was living in a windowless apartment owned by a friend of a friend's parents. The parents didn't seem to understand what we were doing there. The mother would sometimes be sitting in the living area when I got home from work. She'd just sit there, watching me, not saying a word. I spent a lot of time not being there. I spent most of my extra time in a bookstore down the street. The bookstore was open late, which was great, and had a tiny cafe in the back, also great. Since the cafe wasn't visible from the street, not many people actually knew about it, keeping all those WIFI-sucking, table-hoarding freelancers away. Still, nothing.

Jess? I couldn't recall someone named Jess.

There was a phone number. I did the next logical thing: I called the number. Of course, it was disconnected, and I only got an automated message.

Who was Jess?

I had a real problem on my hands. I couldn't sleep, barely ate. I kept turning the question over and over in my head: *Who was Jess?* There was another piece of information that I overlooked. Investigating the photograph carefully, I noticed the bookmark was from the local store I frequented back then called Book Town. The next day, tired from too little sleep, I made my way to my old neighbourhood. Where the store used to be was now a Chipotle. Crap. After eating a burrito, I wrote on my plate in sauce: WHO WAS JESS?

A friend of a friend used to work at Book Town. She worked at the store for almost ten years, so she should know everyone that came through there. This led me to the phone number of the former owner of the store, and I called him up. At first, he couldn't remember anyone named Jess that worked for him or who might have been a customer. I explained the situation, which made me sound like a mentally unfit person. Hope was diminishing by the second when he said, "Wait, I remember someone, but her name was Jessica." He came back on the phone with some old employee records, and I had a full name and address.

Jess, or formally known as Jessica, probably no longer lived at this address, but I had to check it out. Not too far from my place, I came to a large house separated into several apartments. There was an older gentleman at the side of the house installing some wiring. "Excuse me," I said. "Are you the owner of this house?" He nodded, and I went right into it, "Did you ever have a tenant named Jess or Jessica?" I didn't want to explain the entire situation at the moment, but his reply came swiftly. "Who're you, and why do you want to know about Jessica? I mean, no, as long as I've owned this house, I've never had a tenant named, what did you say? Jessica?" He was hiding something, but what? "So, there was someone that lived here named Jessica?" He turned back to his work and said, "I want you off my property. If you don't leave, I'm going to call the police." At that moment, I heard a bang like something was dropped on the floor inside the apartment above. I looked up, and I could see a shadow in the window on the second floor. Someone was listening to our conversation. He looked at me one more time and took out his phone, "I'm calling the cops."

I left, but something happened to Jessica in that house, I'm sure of it. Returning that evening, I walked by to make sure the landlord was not around and climbed the fire escape to the apartment above. The window was slightly open, and someone was inside. I crouched along the wall and listened. The person was talking on the phone, "Yeah, someone was here earlier, and they were asking about Jess. I don't know. What're we going to do?" At that moment, I accidentally knocked over a flower pot. I heard the person running towards the window, so I took off down the fire escape and left the area.

Cutting down an alleyway, I stopped to catch my breath. Doubled over, footsteps approached from around the corner. I cut between two houses and jumped a fence of a neighbouring house. It was rush hour, so when I hit the main street, it was busy enough that I blended in with people on their way home.

After pouring a small glass of whiskey at home, the glass was shaky in my hand as I brought it to my mouth. What the hell happened back there? A quick internet search returned five people with the name Jessica —————. Four of them had active profiles on either Facebook or LinkedIn. One of the Jessica's would have been too young to work at Book Town ten years ago. The other three lived in different countries, and their work history didn't include anything remotely connected to books or stores. The last one seemed to drop off the face of the earth a few years ago. True, she didn't list Book Town as a job, but actually had very little information. To all accounts, she didn't seem to exist anymore. From what I could find, the last place this Jessica lived was the house I just got chased from.

There was no choice, really.

That night, I approached the backyard of the house. The grass hadn't been cut in forever, and a rusted out refrigerator sat in the corner. Movement caught my eye - a raccoon slowly walked along the edge of the fence. We watched each other as we backed away.

From the looks of it, no lights were on in the house. Maybe they were sleeping, but it was early evening. The backdoor was locked, but I tried the window next to it, which slid open. The opening was small, but I managed to squeeze in. As I moved through the house, the one thing I noticed was the lack of furniture. The odd chair. Besides that, it looked like no one lived there.

Slowly, I made my way upstairs to find the same thing: nothing. The flower pots and stuff outside was to create the illusion that someone lived here. I was standing in one of the bedrooms trying to figure out what the hell was going on when car lights shone through the windows. Two men pulled into the driveway and walked towards the front door of the house. There wasn't enough time to get out, so I hid in the closet.

Again, nothing was stored in the closet. I could hear the two men entering the house and walking upstairs. I took out my phone and turned on the flashlight. Something was strange about this closet. The floor had what looked to be scratch marks. Lightly tapping on the wall, it sounded hollow. It didn't take much to push the wall, which moved outwards like a door. Behind it was concrete stairs leading downstairs. Hearing the men coming, I had no choice.

The stairs curved around and seemed to go underground. When I reached the bottom, I found a series of cages. Dungeons. Slowly, I walked past each cell to find them empty. As I neared the last cell, someone pounced, and I jumped back with a yelp. A woman with long hair and a wild look in her eyes reached out for me. She put her finger to her lips, telling me to be quiet, and pointed up at the ceiling.

Wait a second. Recognition.

"Jessica?" I asked.

She shushed me but then nodded.

"What is going on?"

That was when the shovel came smashing down on my head, and the world went dark. When I woke, I was in the far cell down from Jessica. At least I figured out the question that got me here: who was Jess?

~

After our escape, everyone in my life had moved on. Jess and I parted ways. I had no one. Hair long, patchy beard - I spent my days walking the streets, wandering from place to place with no real goal or endpoint.

One day, could have been March, could have been September. I walked into this giant park that runs the entire length of the city. Following a path, I passed a farm and went down a long row of stairs, bringing me deep into a ravine.

I didn't get very far down the path before I reached a 'Do

Not Enter' sign and a fence blocking the way. The sign also said that there was a police presence along the path, and you will be charged for trespassing. No signs like this mattered to me anymore, I was outside the normal ranks of society.

Of course, there was a small slit that other trespassers had made in the fence. So, I crawled through and went on my way down the path. There seemed to be nothing wrong with the area, and I didn't see anything under construction. I came across a half-built bridge, the water stopping at a small makeshift dam. I guess this was the construction zone. I climbed over the top of some giant hills of dirt, and on my way back down the other side, I slipped on a sliver of snow and tumbled the rest of the way down.

My ankle hurt a little bit, but the rest of me seemed okay and intact. A shadow blocked out the sun, and I looked up to find a wiry man offering me his hand. I took it, and he helped me to my feet. He said nothing, only cocked his head towards the path, turned around and walked away. I assumed he wanted me to follow him, so that's what I did.

We walked north along the valley. Every once in awhile, he stopped, turned around and looked to make sure I was still following him. We walked until the sunset. The cold was setting in. Maybe it was even winter, who could tell?

At a certain point along the path, he took a right hand turn into the woods. He stopped at the border between the trees and the path and once again cocked his head to follow. So I did. This was not a good idea. Even though everything worked out, don't do this.

We walked through the bare trees and bushes and came along to a clearing that had a tent leaning beside a fallen tree trunk. A blackened fire pit surrounded by large misshapen rocks was carved into the ground with a dirty lounge chair sitting next to it. The man went over to the other side of the fallen tree - his storage unit? - and pulled out a second lounge chair. He unfolded it and sat it across from the vacant chair. He pointed, and I sat down.

The man went back into his storage unit and started pulling out pieces of wood. He placed them in the fire pit in a decorative pose and quickly got a fire going. He placed a bent up grate across the fire. Two cans of baked beans emerged from his stash, and he put them on the grate.

Then we just sat there watching the fire. We didn't look at each other or talk or anything.

After I don't know how long, he cracked open the cans, handed me one with a spoon, and we ate. We didn't take our eyes off the fire the entire time. When we finished, he took my can and put it into a garbage bag he had beside the storage unit.

We watched the fire some more. We sat there for a long time. At one point, I started shivering, not so much from the cold, but from being so silent and quiet for such a long time. He disappeared into his storage unit once again and emerged holding a blanket, which he tossed over my shoulders. The sun came up, and he stood.

Somehow, all of the items around the fire were able to fit in two bags, one of which he slung over his shoulder. He handed me the other bag. We walked back the way we came, he stopped when at the perimeter of the campsite, looked at me and cocked his head again. I followed him back down the path. Once again, we walked for a very long time. We reached the makeshift dam, I handed him his second bag, and he helped me cross it more gracefully. As I headed back to where I started, I looked back at the wiry man. He stood, watching me. We watched each other for a long time until finally, he raised his hand, waving.

Something overtook me. He headed towards the train

tracks on the other side of the hill. My every being screamed at me to catch up to him, not to lose him, to grab on to him. I looked at the path where I had arrived and saw nothing. Not just saw nothing but saw the future, my future, and only saw emptiness and longing and judgment.

When I caught up to the wiry man, we said nothing. I took his second bag in my hand, and we continued walking along the tracks. Eventually, a train passed, and I followed his lead of how to jump into an empty car - pace yourself alongside it, throw your bag into the car, one hand, the other hand and jump.

Once inside, we laughed with each other, the only sound we'd ever make. Laughter. We spent the next few years never leaving each other's side, moving through the world from one city to another, and never uttering so much as a word.

PART THREE:
TRUE STORIES, I SWEAR!

MY PLACE IN THE WORLD

IN SIX ACTS

ACT ONE

Walking along College Street at the border of the University of Toronto, I came to an intersection where the walking signal was a hand with the palm pointing at me. This means that I am supposed to stop as cars travelling in a perpendicular fashion have the right of way. The opposite of the palm is a profile of a person in mid-step.

Racing along College Street towards this particular intersection was an ambulance. When an ambulance, or any other vehicle equipped with sirens, such as a fire truck or police car, approach a red light, they are required to stop to ensure no other vehicles are moving through the intersection. This ambulance did just that and stopped at the red light.

All cars pulled to the side of the road and pedestrians stood frozen, except for two people who started crossing the street in front of the ambulance. The ambulance began to accelerate through the intersection and abruptly stopped when they saw the pedestrians. These two people, these representatives of an evolved intellectual capacity who showed a unique display of a specific and individualized sense of entitlement, pointed at the symbol of a profile of the person in mid-step and angrily wagged their finger at the ambulance in a staggering act of defiance. Their finger-wagging was letting the ambulance driver know who had the right of way.

And this right of way was with these pedestrians, who then crossed very slowly. In this scenario, they are the

Paul Dore

winners, and the person in the back of the ambulance or the person they were racing to save are the losers.

ACT TWO

For the past few months, I have been trying to eat better. Don't worry, I'm not going to be that person, the one who just because he is leaning towards maybe potentially perhaps becoming vegetarian that he has to tell you and everyone he knows about it.

I'm also exercising more, but I'm not looking to get huge or anything like that. I'm more focused on things like agility, long-distance running, flexibility, cardio — skills that might be needed in the wake of all the political turmoil in the United States. Since it's winter and since I spent a fair amount of my life in arenas, I started skating at various outdoor rinks in city parks.

On this particular day, I decided to take a quick drive to Dufferin Grove Park, which has two ice rinks side-by-side. One dedicated to public skating and the other to hockey. When I arrived at the park, the public skating rink was packed full of kids from the neighbouring school. The hockey rink, on the other hand, had only two people on it, and they were barely moving, mostly chatting and every once in a while, slowly skating down the ice passing a puck.

I put on my figure skates and walked over to the hockey rink. I asked both people on the ice if they would mind if I joined them since the public side was so busy. They replied with big welcoming smiles. And so, the three of us — two hockey players and a figure skater — harmoniously and collectively worked together to stay out of each other's way while accomplishing our individual fitness goals.

Almost finished with my skate, two employees from the park — a man and a woman — approached the hockey rink

80

and yelled at me to come over. She was furious and did most of the talking. At the same time, the man stood behind her with his arms crossed, repeating and highlighting certain aspects of her statements. It was like they took one look at me from their office window and thought, *This guy looks like trouble.*

"You can't be on this rink," she yelled at me. "Can't be on this rink," he said in a low voice, arms crossed, shaking his head. "This ice is for hockey players only," she continued. "Only hockey players," he repeated. "I asked the other two people out here," I said. "They were okay with it." This just made her even more incensed, "You have to leave now!" He said, "Right now." I tried to reason with her: "Okay, let me get this straight. You want me to get off this rink that has two other people on it and go over there that has about twenty kids on it even though we in this community centre have worked quite community-like, sharing this near-empty ice rink."

Now, technically they were right. However, I sensed a fear behind the angry exterior. I figured that they had to keep people like me off the hockey rink. She was scared that there might be scores of figure skaters hiding in the bushes, waiting to take over the hockey rink, waiting for one of their own to sneak on the hockey side. When the time was right, the lone figure skater — she or he — would give the appropriate signal of a split jump or perhaps a very sassy move, and from the bushes would emerge an army of figure skaters, with our ice picks and weird skates and sequins and take over the hockey rink. And the world as we know it would be changed forever.

I was snapped from this image with more yelling from her: "You have to leave right now!" So, I left, but the joke was on her. The ex-president of the United States of America believes climate change is a hoax created by China to make US manufacturing non-competitive. Climate change is real, and the precious ice that makes up her hockey rink will be melting a little earlier every year. So, I win. We all lose, but I win.

ACT THREE

I enjoy going to the theatre because of the art, the writing, the acting and so on, but really because plays start on time. I've been to some music shows, and other performing arts shows that start an hour or more after the official appointment. I understand this is so the audience can arrive and get settled and all that. The general excuse for the tardiness is — well, *Everyone knows the show will start late*. The audience knows this, the show producers know this. We've created a system that fails on both sides.

This particular play I was at did not start on time. The crowd seemed a bit older, and there were lots of steps, so I forgave this divergence from the norm. One of the younger patrons found his seat a few rows in front of me, removed his jacket, and I noticed that he wore the same shirt as me. It was not like I noticed he was wearing the same *white* shirt as me. In fact, it was a unique and sophisticated design. One of a kind, or so I thought. My point is that it was a somewhat unusual shirt. I just took note of this as a coincidence and moved my intention to the performance.

Since the play was unnecessarily three hours long, there were two intermissions. During the first intermission, there was a lineup for the washroom. As the line moved forward, I realized that the gentleman who had the same shirt as me - let's call him Same Shirt - was at the urinal. There were only two urinals and a few stalls, all were taken. The man at the urinal beside Same Shirt finished. I was second in line, and I felt okay about this situation because I could change places with Same Shirt, like we were tagging out in a wrestling match.

The guy in front of me wasn't moving towards that now empty urinal beside Same Shirt. He was waiting for a stall. So, I walked up to the urinal, and in a crowd of about 200 theatre-goers, two people who had the same unusual shirt on were now peeing next to each other. I was hoping that no one would say anything, but there's a comedian in every crowd, and this other guy waiting in line said, "Hey, you two are wearing the same shirt!"

Same Shirt finished up, and as he turned, he saw me in my shirt but also his shirt and was confused because he didn't know that I had stepped up to the urinal beside him. As Same Shirt washed his hands, the comedian in line now repeated what was quickly becoming his catchphrase: "Hey, you guys are wearing the same shirt!" He followed it up with, "Hey, are you two related or something?" Okay, let's say Same Shirt and I were related and let's say that we saw an advertisement for this play and really wanted to see it. We picked a date and bought tickets. On the day of the show, I called this relative of mine, maybe a brother or a cousin and said, "Hey, you know what we should do? We should both wear that unique shirt we've got because I think it would be cool if we both walked around in public wearing the same thing. That makes a lot of sense and something we should definitely do. And then we can time it so we're peeing next to each other just to see if we could blow someone's mind!"

As I washed my hands, the comedian in line wanted to make sure that I heard his earlier statement, "Hey, you had the same shirt as that other guy!"

At the end of the show, I put on my coat and zipped it up. I located the position of the guy wearing the same shirt as me because now I had to manage my movements in relation to his. I don't know who won in that scenario. It definitely wasn't me or the guy who wore the same shirt as me. He'll probably never wear this shirt again, and I burned that fucking shirt after that night. I think the winner here was the comedian in line, who will probably be telling this story to people for years to come.

ACT FOUR

Riding my bike down Bloor Street West, I came to a red light at Dufferin Street. There was a lot of traffic, and I was at the front of a long line of bikers. Beside me was a man driving a white Toyota Corolla.

I want to interject here for a moment and ask you a question. Whenever an emergency vehicle, such as an ambulance or fire truck, needs to get somewhere in a hurry, the paramedics turn on bright flashing lights and loud sirens. These are to let everyone around them know that they are in a real hurry and getting to their destination promptly is essential. We're all familiar with that, correct? Good.

I heard the ambulance sirens from a long way back. Whether in my car or on my bike, whenever I heard sirens, I just pulled to the side of the road, you know, to get out of the way. Since I was already by the side of the road, when the light turned green, I just stayed put.

Behind me, the cars jockeyed for positions left and right. As the ambulance approached the intersection, the only person that didn't move was the man in the white Corolla. He patiently waited at the red light, oblivious to anything happening around him.

The ambulance couldn't fit around the white Corolla, and there it sat with sirens blaring and lights flashing. I knocked on the driver's window and yelled, "You have to move!" But he just looked at me confusingly. I pointed behind him, and he sat up straight in shock like the ambulance snuck up on him.

Similar to Act One, the person in the back of the ambulance or the person they were racing to save are the losers. There is no clear winner here.

ACT FIVE

As I mentioned in Act Two, I have been trying to exercise more. I started swimming laps at my local community centre pool. I've been in a lot of pools over the years and noticed a pattern. Usually, there are three lanes for laps: slow, medium and fast. Men, and in my very scientific study, it's always men 100% of the time, enter the pool and jump right into the fast lane. They may not be the fastest swimmers, in fact, a lot of the time they are barely treading water, but in their mind? In their mind, they are 23-time Olympic gold medallist swimmer Michael Phelps.

Because of this phenomenon, the fast lane is usually loaded down with slow-moving men, leaving the other lanes open. Many times, five to seven men duke it out — slowly — in the fast lane, while I have a relaxing time in the medium lane.

A couple of weeks ago, the pool was quite busy. Some of the men were forced to take the hit to their ego and do their laps in the medium lane. I jumped in and stood at the end of the pool, getting my goggles on. Beside me was an older lady doing some kind of water aerobics.

A man was swimming towards us. He stopped and stood, raising his goggles. I recognized him as a Michael Phelps right away. "Hey! You know, it's very difficult for us to do our laps when all of you are standing at the end of the pool in our way. You're not supposed to be standing there, it's against the rules." I looked at the older woman doing water aerobics, but she just shrugged her shoulders.

As Michael Phelps stood yelling, there was another swimmer behind him approaching and not paying attention. Now, I could have alerted Michael Phelps that this swimmer was coming up behind him. But then I thought: *No, you know what? Perhaps this could be a teaching point for him.* He kept yelling, "It's really difficult for us to turn quickly when-"

-he didn't get a chance to finish. That other determined swimmer somehow managed to bump into his legs, causing Michael Phelps — as though he was sitting on a dunk tank — to plunge completely underwater.

Unlike Act Four, there is a loser and winner. Michael Phelps is the obvious loser, and I clearly emerge as the gold medal winner.

ACT SIX

I can be judgmental. I don't suffer fools lightly. But I try to be patient. I live in a condo building, and my bike is held in a cage with everyone else's bike down in the parking garage. Residents register bikes, and we each get a key for the padlock on the front gate. The fence and gate are made up of small mesh-like squares.

I was going out for one of my epic rides and knew that my tires needed pumping up. I brought my bike pump down into the cage and was inflating the tires when a man and woman approached. He might, in modern vernacular, be what one might call a 'bro.' He marched right up to me and said: "Do you have a tool that could loosen my bike seat?" I'm not usually the kind of guy that you look at and say: *Now that guy. That guy is a person who carries an array of specialized tools.* When I replied in the negative, he said,

"I just asked because you had a bike pump." Which, okay, sort of a stretch, but one that I understood.

He left the bike cage, and I watched as he proceeded to close the gate and put the padlock on, essentially locking me inside. Well, not essentially, like actually locking me inside. I said, "No, please, don't do that." He said, "Why not?" I walked over to the gate. "You see, if you lock the gate, I am locked inside and can't get out." He looked at me with blank eyes and said, "But, you have a key." After a pause, "Yes, but as you can see, I can't reach through and unlock the gate from the inside." I stuck my fingers through the cage to display my inability to reach the lock.

He continued, "But it's the rules. I have to lock the gate." I looked at his companion for help. I assumed this was his girlfriend and that this display of confusion must have been a big part of their relationship. She had earbuds in, ignoring both of us. She was just probably glad that someone else had to deal with him.

Then I imagined him just leaving me there, locked in the cage. It was autumn and people weren't biking as much. The cage was in the parking lot, and so cell phone reception was spotty. I couldn't even call for help.

But -

- there was so much more that I wanted to do with my life. I wanted to meet that special someone and grow old with her. I was close to finishing this book you are reading right now. I'm pretty sure that I don't want to have kids, but maybe, like everyone tells me, I just haven't met the right person yet. Instead, my life would be cut short — it might be months until my body was found, all shrivelled after slowly dying of starvation.

But then he just shrugged, unlocked the gate and walked away. Unfortunately, I would have to name the girlfriend as the loser in the scenario, as she voluntarily opted into a relationship with this guy. On the flip side of that, and also, unfortunately, the bro is the winner, as he somehow found someone willing to form a romantic partnership with him.

MOUNTAIN FOG

The flight was direct from Toronto to Beijing. After 18 hours of recycling my own oxygen and the oxygen of the other passengers, we were released, unleashed into the chaos of Beijing's airport.

The weeks leading up to my trip were hectic, full of long working days trying to finish projects. I edited right up to a few hours before my flight, leaving an interviewee from a documentary in mid-sentence. Usually, I am much more prepared for travel. Accommodations booked, attractions well documented. These arrangements were primarily done over the Internet, but since at the time China was still somewhat restricted online, the opportunity to book beforehand was limited. I decided to improvise.

After picking up my bag, I elbowed through the crowd and approached a hotel-booking booth. I reserved a room and was given a business card with the name written in Chinese characters. I was instructed to take a bus to the main train station and from there, get in a taxi, present the card to the driver who would then take me to the hotel. Easy, right? The reality: I was a dumbass from the start.

Outside, a rainstorm in full swing. Later on, people told me that after weeks of nothing but sun and forty-degree weather, the humidity broke, and the rain started. Torrential rain, on the exact day I arrived. Somehow I found the proper bus, and we drove into the heart of Beijing. On the bus, two middle-aged businessmen tried to talk with me. We carried on an entire conversation speaking two different languages. They seemed happy, getting excited at some points, quiet and displaying thoughtful looks at other times.

The bus stopped outside the train station. I stepped into

a puddle up to my ankles and three young women holding umbrellas swarmed. They flashed brochures of various hotels in my face and spoke rapid-fire, gesticulating with arms. I waved them off, smugly said in English, "No thanks, I've already got a place to stay!"

The outside of the train station was a vast hangar-sized open area with the building running along an entire block. People lined the length of the station using the canopy as shelter from the rain. They just stood, waiting. The rain did not allow me to survey the scene, I was quickly soaked to the bone.

I located the taxi stand and ran through the rain. In the first taxi, I smiled and handed the driver the business card. Leaned back, looking forward to finding my dry hotel room. I would learn to drop the smugness quickly. He examined the card, flipped it over, reread it. He was perplexed, brow furrowed, shook his head. He handed the card right back and waved me out of his car. Pushed me back into the rain. The taxi next in line did the same. And the one after that didn't even let me get into the car.

Standing in the pouring rain, I decided to join the people under the canopy at the train station. Review my options, develop a new plan of action. It might have been my imagination, but it felt like the intensity of the rain increased. I ran across the promenade, my backpack straining my shoulders.

I found a space under the canopy. People stared. At this particular moment, I felt they were all wondering, *What in the hell is this guy doing here?* I was thinking along the same lines.

Once I stopped for a moment – and perhaps due to all this water – my bladder informed me it needed draining. As I moved through the thick crowd, my bulky backpack bounced and bumped into people. Through a window, I saw the international symbol for washrooms, but you were not allowed inside the train station unless you had a ticket. I shook away the thought of buying a ticket just to use the washroom. The same washroom sign was visible by the corner of the building.

Now I understood what everyone else was standing and staring at – waiting as they figured out what to do next. I was already wet, so I just walked right out from under the canopy and into the rain. I couldn't run anymore. I imagined someone having a good laugh watching me zigzag from the bus stop to the train station to the taxi stand and back to the train station as though I was inside some elaborate, life-sized video game. Perhaps this was as far as I'd get, my remaining time here trying to get a taxi.

Back where I started: the bus stop. The young women holding the umbrellas and brochures were waiting for another bus. Soaking, I approached them. Any hint of my earlier smugness seeped away with the rain. Through the flurry of arms and brochures, I said, "If you can get me a taxi, I'll stay at your hotel." They might not have understood my words, but they understood my desperation. One girl instantly motioned for me to follow, and we ran. Cars honked as we cut across roads, between vehicles and splashed through puddles. We got into the first taxi, the driver remembered me, started to wave me back out. But my saviour, the young woman, yelled right back at him. Pointed straight ahead through the windshield.

Driving in Beijing was organized chaos. The pattern of the taxi driver was gas-honk-brake-yell at other drivers, and any number of variations of those four elements. We drove for about ten minutes, turning and weaving through so many roads that my internal compass barely recognized my own reflection in the rearview mirror. We pulled up to a ramshackle hotel and ran into the lobby. I booked a room, paid for it, and the young woman bowed and ran back into the rain, probably returning to the bus stop.

I found my room, used the washroom and collapsed on the bed. Woke up the next morning, not remembering what country I was in. I looked out the window at the city. China. Somewhere in Beijing. But where?

~

The first thing I do in a new city is go exploring, get my bearings. There were no bearings in Beijing and no familiar reference points. This was clearly uncharted waters.

Beijing was a stunning metropolis packed with cars, people, bicycles, food carts, sellers, buyers and more people. Every once in a while, I would have to find a place with no people and just sit down. The notion of personal space went out the window.

I walked through busy streets, rode the packed subway and found the largest park in the city. Once through the gates, the noise of the streets dissipated, disappeared, and calmness reigned. Groups of people practiced tai chi, ballroom dancing, flew kites and played a game similar to hacky sack.

At the other end of the park, I was thrust back into the noise and congestion. I found Tiananmen Square, the vast area where decades ago, people protested, and violence against citizens would always be remembered. Now it was full of tourists like me.

To cross some roads, there were pedestrian tunnels that went underground. At a main intersection, I stepped down the steps and found rows and rows of people sitting on the ground selling everything from food to DVDs to crafts. Each product rested on cloth-like material with wooden sticks on either end.

As I moved through the crowd, I saw it come like a wave. From the other side of the tunnel, a message was being passed. One by one, like dominoes, each seller grabbed the wooden sticks, turning the cloth into a carrying-case, packing their products in the makeshift bag and bolting to the entrance of the tunnel behind me. Within thirty seconds, the tunnel was completely deserted except for me. At the other end, a lonely police officer strolled into view, stopped and squinted at me. I smiled and took a few steps back towards the entrance of the tunnel. I looked to my right, and along the steps all the way up to the street, the sellers were hiding. They looked at me wide-eyed, the one closest to me putting index finger to lips, asking me to be quiet. I turned back to the officer, smiled and ran up the stairs.

I walked down Tiananmen Square towards the large portrait of Mao Zedong hanging above The Forbidden City. Perhaps I would find what I'm looking for there locked away. What was it I was looking for on this trip? Why had I travelled halfway across the world? A response to some spiritual crisis?

Before I could answer this, a young woman who said she was an art student came up to me and asked if she could practice her English. She steered me towards a gallery where she wanted to show me some of her work. The gallery was really nice, but that was when the selling started.

I got out of there without buying anything, but the art student was still at my side. I couldn't shake her. I went into a bookstore, she followed. I went into a shopping mall, thought I lost her, then she emerged at the exit. She wanted to show me an authentic Chinese tea experience.

A few blocks later, we went into a department store-like building, and on the third floor, we entered the authentic Chinese teashop. It resembled a high-end office with mahogany floors and walls. A woman sat behind a large desk, and we took two chairs opposite her. It felt like an interview for a job that I was clearly unqualified for.

A well-dressed man came in with different types of tea. The woman behind the desk - let's call her The Boss - explained the benefits of the tea. My art student friend translated.

Oolong tea originally means black dragon tea and is produced by a process involving withering under the intense sun and oxidation enabling curling and twisting of the leaves. Helps to lower blood pressure, encourages weight loss and reduces cholesterol. Chrysanthemum teas, such as Yellow Mountain Tribute, helps with recovery from influenza, acne and are good for the liver. Good old-fashioned green tea such as Snail Spring is linked to studies showing reduced risks of different forms of cancer.

After my tea experience, I made my way back to Mao Zedong and The Forbidden City. I entered the city, Mao looming over the entrance, judging me, and I walked across the stone pathways. A giant city within a city. Red walls surrounded the buildings with vast areas between each successive temple. In Beijing, people were everywhere, but here, there was so much space, too much space, and people respectively whispered, not wanting the ghosts to hear their modern words. I veered off the path, crossed some imaginary line where the air was captured, catapulted away, and you heard the beating of your heart, and everyone seemed so very distant.

Perhaps this was what I looked for - to move internally into myself, understand more the relationship of my mind, my body, my heart and my thoughts? Connect to some type of past life and experience a completely different sense of historical context.

The Forbidden City consisted of 980 buildings with 8707 bays of rooms and was the imperial palace from the Ming Dynasty to the end of the Qing Dynasty. The City was built over 500 years ago. This notion of history, not only one or two hundred years old, but centuries-old, was like nothing I had ever experienced. With each step, there was a discovery of a new century.

I spent hours in The Forbidden City, stepped from one era to another. Honing in on some profound inner-sanctum, a sense of connecting to history, perhaps not one that was my own, one that was complicated and at times horrific, but for me it meant something important, vital.

The last temple was the oldest, and I stopped. The final building was a gift shop. Beside the gift shop was a Starbucks. Inside The Forbidden City, after walking through all this history, was a Starbucks. I looked from the ancient temples to this modern temple. The profundity disappeared, but a clarity ignited inside my brain. Maybe not so much a clarity as a craving.

I went inside Starbucks and enjoyed a comforting coffee in a different sort of temple.

~

Twenty hours on a train.

Go home, open a closet, clean out all the contents. Wait, not the closest - the nook. The useless storage space nook under the stairs, the one with the slanted ceiling. Leave the bare bulb on, take only what you can fit on your person. One bottle of water and a cardboard cup of dried ramen noodles allowed. Close the door, stand, stooped over and set your watch to count down twenty hours. Look at your watch every five minutes. Over time, the minute hand will seem to go backwards rather than forwards. You realize a gap has ripped open in the space-time continuum, and you have entered a black hole. This was your brain after ten hours. After fifteen hours, hallucinations set in. After eighteen, suicide by self-inflicted punches to the head became a realistic option.

Eventually, the train arrived at my destination. After staying in Beijing for a couple of weeks, I welcomed the clean early morning air of the small town. If I knew where I was - my body was still on the train, my insides continuing with the forward motion.

In my travels, I'm drawn to mountains. Germany, Switzerland, New Zealand, Austria. Almost every place I've visited, I made sure there was a stop atop a mountain. In China, that meant taking a train out of the metropolis, but unlike Europe, where you could be in a completely different country inside two hours, the sheer magnitude of space in China meant longer travel times. Twenty hours long.

I decided to get to the hotel on my own. It had sort of worked so far. The hotel was located in the heart of Tai'an, at the foot of one of China's five sacred peaks - Mount Tai. An ancient cement staircase wound up the mountain - 6293 steps to be exact - and my plan was to climb every one of them. But not today. Today I would relax, take a hike around the mountain and through the tree-lined slope that led to a valley.

The mountain rose from the ground towards the sky. Through a gated entrance, the path split in two. According to my map, the path veering to the left led around the mountain and offered a four-hour hike. Trees lined the way, the sun shone on my shoulders.

About an hour into the hike, Buddha appeared. As Buddha's head bobbed closer, I stepped aside to allow four men carrying on their shoulders a life-sized golden statue of the suffering representative of the noble truth. What did this mean? My usual selfish disposition decreed these men carried this statue at this moment because they knew I was hiking. It must be a sign, but of what? After walking some more, I came across a temple under renovations. Buddha, apparently, was upgrading.

The only other person I encountered was an old man. He approached fast, caught up to me and fell in beside my steps. Grey-haired buzz cut, deeply tanned skin, he held his shirt in his hand, his bare upper body revealing a thick muscular torso. He said nothing, only smiled. We walked briskly for a while until we came to a rolling stream. I stopped, sat on a rock, hoping he continued on. We couldn't speak to each other, but the silence was even more awkward.

He was a different kind of Buddha. Animated. Tanned instead of golden. And one who wouldn't take no for an answer. I shrugged to myself – just a bit of local Chinese hospitality wanting to show me the sights.

Buddha motioned for me to get up. The sound of his voice alarmed me. My only comfort thus far being that we didn't have to talk. He broke the contract. Buddha grabbed my arm, pulled me to my feet. Emphatically pointed at me, pointed at the path. We started up again, faster. Speed walking turned into jogging, jogging turned into running.

The path was not flat land. I didn't notice at first because the path travelled on a slight upward incline. Slight being the operative word, but incline being the more important one. My feet didn't notice because they were just trying to keep up. My lungs didn't notice because they were busy trying to breathe. If I stopped, Buddha rolled his eyes. He grew impatient. We climbed higher and higher. The trail cut through people's backyards: small stretches of gardens, chickens crossing our path, small children playing who stopped and regarded us as a strange pair.

Lost track of time, almost like I was back on the train. Almost. Buddha ran up ahead of me. The path seemed to just end. Buddha leapt off the end of the trail. I sprinted to catch up, and it was almost too late. The path ended all right - ended in a drop straight down the side of a cliff. I put the brakes on, slid across the dirt, tiny pebbles kicked over the edge, pinged on the jagged rocks at the bottom. The momentum of my body torqued over my feet, and I went head first over the side, grasping for something, anything, my hand grabbed at the ground, stopped the forward motion, my head peeked past the ledge, and I stared straight down the cliff.

My eyes scanned for the Buddha's body. I heard his voice from above - was he in heaven already? Was there a heaven? I rolled around on to my back. Beside me was a boulder, a rock wall raised five stories. Along the side of the boulder, metal handles cascaded, enabled a climber - if he or she so inclined - to capture the full extent of the view. The catch was the handles spiralled along the side of the boulder facing the drop off the cliff. In my opinion, a major design flaw.

Buddha poked his head out from the top of the boulder. He leapt off where I was sprawled, had scaled the metal handled ladder. He motioned for me to follow, smiled, pointed to the view. A thought occurred to me: *no one knew I was here*. Sure, friends and family knew I was in China, but China is big. Buddha could chuck me right from this cliff, I could disappear, and no one would know.

Working on automatic pilot, beyond tired, my legs picked me up, and I ran down the path. I heard Buddha's footsteps running after me. I stopped when my lungs felt like they were going to explode. Doubled over, I heard footsteps.

I ran as far as my legs moved me, but didn't understand why this was even happening. Maybe he was just trying to help me get some exercise? The path seemed so much longer than when we went up. Along the stream, where the foliage grew denser, my lungs couldn't take anymore. I leapt from the path, crawled under a bush. Focused on slowing my heart rate, concentrated on controlling my breathing.

Footsteps. He stopped, listened. He stood on the path right in front of the bush. Scanned the trees. I watched him through a space in the bush. Finally, he kept running down the path.

I waited and did not move from the bush for two hours, making sure he wasn't coming back. As the sun lowered over the horizon, I emerged, walked with tired steps down the path.

~

The next day, I was determined to walk up the 6293 steps of Mount Tai in a much more direct way. And alone, which wasn't in the cards for me. When I almost reached the entrance to the foot of the mountain, a young man approached me, wanting to practice his English. He seemed harmless, and so we started up the path towards the steps.

The young man was a student and said he walked up the mountain once a week. He spent most of his time alone studying, and the mountain hike provided exercise for both his body and mind. As we walked, he told me about the history of the mountain.

Mount Taishan is one of five sacred Taoist mountains in China. For over 3000 years, Chinese emperors of various dynasties made pilgrimages to Taishan. Confucius composed poetry and prose on the mountain and stone inscriptions, tablets and temples remain as testaments to these visits. Right up the centre of the mountain was the flight of stone steps. We took our first steps and had only 6292 more.

I was not a leader of men looking to prove myself through this pilgrimage up the mountain. But perhaps I would find something here, that something which seemed to elude me during the trip thus far. At the very least, I hoped I would not climb all these steps only to find a Starbucks at the summit.

The sun was out, the day was humid. The air turned cooler as we went higher. The steps were old, the stone cracked. The path was wide and snaked up the side of the mountain. I tried not to think of the difficulties of forming these steps and why, after thousands of years, the purpose of the steps at this particular moment was to bring a tourist such as myself with white, untanned legs to the top.

We came upon a middle-aged man helping an elderly woman up the steps. He kept putting his hand on her arm to help, and she kept brushing him away. She wanted to make it to the top on her own. They were far behind us after only a short time and figured they would be at it for a while. They seemed okay with that.

We climbed beside a man that was bringing supplies to the restaurant on the summit. He had a wooden staff across his shoulders. On either side of the wooden staff hung a crate of glass water bottles. There was another man about 20 steps ahead of him with a similar load. They walked slow but steady. Every day they brought supplies up the mountain in this way. A groove in their shoulder muscles had been worked in from the wooden staff. This was their job. Every day.

I was tiring as we reached the halfway point. The student

asked vibrant questions about my life in Canada. After much talking, he came to the topic I believed he really wanted to know about. He asked if I had a girlfriend and wanted to know about all my relationships.

"There is a girl that I really like," he said, "but there's nothing I can do about it."

"What's love got to do with it?" I asked. "You have to get to know someone before that stage. Just talk to her."

"I must finish my studies," he said. "Then get a job and then perhaps I can fall in love."

As my body, legs and feet tired, I think he grew tired of me. As I rested next to a temple built along the side of the mountain, the student continued on, we parted ways, and I hoped I didn't complicate his view of love.

After my break, I returned to the steps until finally, I neared the top. The stairs turned almost completely vertical at this point, and my legs were barely functional. It looked as though the stairs led right up to the deep blue sky. I summoned energy from somewhere and ran up the remaining steps, jumped across the threshold and landed at the top in a billow of dust and dirt. I crawled over to the side of the path and just sat there for who knows how long.

Something shiny caught my eye. The sun's rays reflected off a piece of metal buried in the dirt. I brushed the dust aside, picked up a small silver amulet that resembled a traditional Chinese dress. This amulet had a story all to itself, but for now, it became a symbol of my triumphant climb.

Clouds were on the horizon. Not dark clouds, just enough to create an overcast. I've learned from previous experiences that the weather on top of mountains can change in an instant.

My first mountain was in Oberstdorf, Germany. I

accompanied my father on a business trip, and we ended up in the small town in the mountains. We rode the trolley up, and at the top, I was left alone. A fog rolled in, surrounding me, and I remembered a silence so deafening, a silence that was only penetrated by rocks falling off the cliff and slamming below. Everyone disappeared, and I never felt so lonely, but it was a calm loneliness.

Ten years later, I returned to this same mountain in Oberstdorf by myself. On that sunny day, I rode the trolley and the higher I got, the faster the clouds rolled in. At the top, a fog followed - the same fog? - and the calmness and the silence returned.

Back on Mount Tai, I followed a path that wound around the summit. As I walked, the clouds continued to roll in. I reached a lookout point, and no one was around. The fog moved swiftly, surrounding me. The movement of the fog brought silence, and everything disappeared. I heard a word, a vibration coming from the ground beneath my feet, emanating from the trees, from the rocks. The word I heard was a unity of silence, a word spoken in the wind, condensed in the fog, hidden away and only visible when surrounded by nothing, only visible when mortality and the impermanence of places and things ceased. The word I heard made a sound but made no sound at all. It was transferred to me from the trees and the rocks and the fog.

TRAGIC OPTIMISM

The sound of the car slamming into bones bounced off the street. An empty skateboard rolled past me as people ran on to the road, and other cars stopped with a screech. Heading up Castro Street, I took a hard right onto Market. I was walking uphill towards the water when I saw the skateboarder rolling fast downhill towards the intersection. I don't want to blame the victim, but he was clearly out of control and going full speed into traffic. I mean, what the hell else did he think was going to happen?

With impeccable timing, a car approached perpendicularly, smoking the skateboarder. There was no time to warn the guy, and I don't think it would've even mattered, he had made his decision. And so, on my second day away in the middle of a sunny afternoon, I watched a man go flying over the hood of a car as his skateboard made the rest of the trek downhill.

Welcome to San Francisco.

Maybe it was because I was getting older, but I started booking flights as early as I could get them. It meant takeoffs at ridiculous times like seven in the morning. Which meant getting to the airport in the middle of the night. Which meant trying to figure out a way to actually get to the airport in the middle of the night. Instead — and trust me, I never would have considered this before turning forty — I take the last train to the airport the night before and hang out in the airport until the gates open. It's fun, in a sadistic sort of way.

Have you ever been in an airport overnight? The first time I did this, I thought it might be exciting. I pretended that I was on the run, maybe like in an action movie or something, and I had to sneak out of the city. Bad guys were on the lookout, and I had to slip by them and escape to some exotic international location. My girlfriend arrived at the exotic international location via a different route, we didn't know if we'd make it, didn't know when we parted ways days earlier whether we'd see each other again. But we made it. Credits rolled as we strolled along the beach.

It was actually really boring because nobody cared that you were there. It was just kind of sad. Nobody really wanted to be there, and people were trying to sleep in all manner of uncomfortable ways. I liked it because if I was ever good at something, it was being in one place for long periods. I knew how to entertain myself because my stupid brain never stopped working.

Whenever I passed through customs, I usually had the feeling like I was going to be invited into some side room and interrogated for several hours. I have two passports, which at times made me feel like an actual person on the run, and figured someone was going to put an end to all this. I didn't know why as everything was above board and legitimate, I just usually felt like I didn't belong no matter where I hung my hat. Even though I very much belonged. Especially in those places where I very much belonged.

Since I rounded forty, I also always checked my bag. I didn't want to be bothered with it, and it saved me from having to fight for space in the overhead compartment. Even though I had to wait for my luggage on the other end, and I run the genuine risk of losing it along the way, I doubled down on this risk rather than having to cart it around with me everywhere and make sure my liquids were less than the required amount.

In addition to being able to entertain myself, I could sleep almost anywhere. This meant getting an hour or two of sleep sitting upright in an uncomfortable airplane seat was no problem. Sure, I had to work out a few kinks in my neck afterwards, but it was worth it.

For some reason, I get very emotional when flying. I don't know why but recently learned that this was an actual thing that happened to a lot of people. I could be watching *John Wick* and really get all worked up when his dog died. I was absolutely sure no one around me noticed. I read that when flying, some people really felt close to their mortality, and so got all weepy-eyed. I just think it was the air pressure.

Since San Francisco is a ridiculously expensive city, I was staying slightly outside the downtown core. I actually planned it this way because I could walk from the airport to where I would be laying my head for the next week. As you may have guessed, my flight back home was even earlier, and I wanted to be able to get to the airport on my own.

There was something about making my own way from the airport to where I was staying. A challenge. I was sleepy, even though I napped, and it was the first time I'd have to navigate this new city. Even though I have a relatively terrible sense of direction, I enjoy trying to figure it out.

Generally speaking, airports aren't built to walk in and out of. Security reasons, probably. Still, I made my way out along a road that I most likely should not have been walking along. It was basically a four-lane highway, but there was a sidewalk. At every intersection, I expected the sidewalk to end and for my journey to come to a close before it even got started. Even through construction zones, there was still an accessible walkway. A few times, it was dicey. Plus, it was a Sunday, so not much was happening.

I knew very little about the area that I was staying in, and I couldn't wait until I got settled. It was tough to blend in with a trolley bag. It screamed tourist. It was also loud on sidewalks and drew unwanted attention. Besides being able to walk from the airport, I picked this place to stay because I could check-in entirely on my own. I didn't need to make small talk with the host and could just get things started.

When travelling, I was always amazed when things worked out. From the check-in at the airport to getting through customs to gaining access to where I was staying. It still amazed me. The place where I was staying had two doors — a garage code and a code for the inside door. The first code opened the garage door. Amazing. Then the second code also worked, and I was inside. I mean, come on, blows me away every time.

I'm not picky when it comes to where I stay. In fact, I like small compact places. Give me enough room to organize my things, a bed to sleep on and a desk to sit at to read and write, and I'm a damn happy fool. My room had all those fixings and more. I unpacked and headed straight out to do two things — figure out the subway system and see the ocean.

One of my favourite things to do when travelling was to ride public transit like I had lived there for many years. I was staying about a ten-minute walk from a Bay Area Rapid Transit (BART) station, and when I got there, I hung back.

Watched.

Obviously, I had read up on how it works, but even though every public transit system does the same thing — got you from here to there — they all operated just a little bit different. After a few minutes, I figured it out, used a machine to get a refillable card, loaded it up, and swiped my way through the turnstile. The train was fast, as we sped through the tunnel, the structure shook like the very things holding it together were coming apart at the seams.

At the other end, I walked out into the warm downtown air and saw the ocean in the distance. People were everywhere, and I joined the crowd. I had no idea where I was going, except to head towards the water. I took a hard left and walked along the coast. The Golden Gate Bridge was in the distance, and after spending the night at the airport, and being all cramped, it was great to be free. I weaved my way along the waterfront, climbed a few hills, and cut across the city. After all the energy it took to get here, I was really running on empty. It was time to go home.

Back at my place, beside the bed, was a short row of books. Mostly business and travel books, except for one: *Man's Search for Meaning* by Victor Frankl. I had a copy of this for years but never read it. The title scared me. Some books were forgettable, others followed you around. As I rested my sore feet, I cracked open the book. As I drifted off to sleep, I dreamed about Tragic Optimism: "The world is in a bad state, but everything will become still worse unless each of us does their best."

My mission for the next day was to hit up the Mission District. Ever since *You Shall Know Our Velocity!* Dave Eggers has been a considerable influence on me. Especially with how he used his status to do other things, such as help start 826 Valencia (from their website): "An [international] organization dedicated to supporting under-resourced students ages six to eighteen with their creative and expository writing skills and to helping teachers inspire their students to write. Services are structured around the understanding that great leaps in learning can happen with one-on-one attention and that strong writing skills are fundamental to future success." And here I was on Valencia Street! I just wanted to see the physical building and make sure it actually existed. I loved that places like this lived in the world, it helped things be less worse. I felt it was full of individuals doing their best.

A good feeling to have until you were walking down the street and watched a man get hit by a car. The crunch. The lonely skateboard. Somehow, the guy didn't seem that hurt. He got up as though this was something that happened all the time, limped over to the sidewalk, and sat down on the curb. I had picked up his skateboard, walked over, and handed it to him. He thanked me as a crowd formed around him. He rubbed his neck but insisted that he was okay.

I continued into the Castro District. I believed that a place held on to its history, and I had always been fascinated by Harvey Milk and all that happened here. Although it was only mid-morning, when I hit the main strip, there was a tall man standing at the corner dressed in head to toe leather and smoking a thick cigar. I smiled at him and he nodded. I visited the Gay, Lesbian, Bisexual, and Transgender Historical Society Museum. The small but powerful exhibit ended with one of the last recordings Harvey Milk made before he died. He made it because he knew that his life was in danger. These words, sadly, still apply today:

"I fully realize that a person who stands for what I stand for — an activist, a gay activist — becomes the target or potential target for a person who is insecure, terrified, afraid or very disturbed. Almost everything that was done was done with an eye on the gay movement. I cannot prevent some people from feeling angry and frustrated and mad in response to my death, but I hope they will take the frustration and madness and instead of demonstrating or anything of that type, I would hope that they would take the power and I would hope that five, ten, one hundred, a thousand would rise. All I ask is for the movement to continue, and if a bullet should enter my brain, let that bullet destroy every closet door."

My intention with a trip like this was to just hang out. I

wasn't in the mood to really do much except walk around in the warm weather, drink good coffee, read, and write. I'd be in San Francisco for New Year's Eve, and I must admit that this was totally fine with me. I gave up on New Year's Eve a long time ago. For this year, I ended up heading back to the place I was staying early, having been tuckered out after a long day of walking up and down steep hills.

The last time I had fun on New Year's Eve was almost ten years ago when I was in Berlin. I had never seen anything like it up to that point, and nothing like it since. It was mass chaos out in the streets, complete with people passed out on the sidewalk. Others ignited cherry bombs and threw them into the subway as the doors closed. I watched a man climb down on to the subway tracks to retrieve a fallen half-bottle of vodka. A train was coming in the distance and came closer at an alarmingly fast speed. A friend of a friend lived in Berlin, and I followed her around for half the night going in and out of dodgy night clubs, one of them had an entrance under a bridge that looked like an abandoned building. After losing her and striking out on my own, I watched a man dropkick another man. I witnessed the most amount of vomit emanating out of people I had ever seen in my life. I mean, that was it — what could possibly top that?

Anyway, I digress. It was not nearly as exciting in San Francisco. As I walked home, some mild fireworks went off in the distance. New Year's Eve was for couples being together and kissing at midnight. There was no one around to kiss me. I was in bed by 10:00 pm, which was fine with me.

I'd be returning the day before my birthday, which fell on a Monday, and which was an entirely useless time to celebrate anything. So, I set aside an entire day in San Francisco to just do exactly every stupid thing I enjoy all at once.

I woke up early in the morning and went for a ridiculously large breakfast at the IHOP down the street. During my 20s, I went through a significant obsession, as a lot of sensitively-minded young men do, with the Beat Generation. Kerouac was my guy, but also like a lot (or at least most) sensitively-minded young men, I grew out of this phase. That being said, I still found the famous City Lights bookstore and bought myself a book. I believed that spaces held history, and many in the literary world from that time walked through those doors. I didn't know what it was, but I felt something. Ghosts, maybe?

To finish the day, all I wanted to do was just go for a long walk. Close to where I was staying, there was a park that was a two for one: it was a — modest — mountain with hiking trails. I always liked me a good mountain I could walk up. When I entered the park, there was a sign on the fence: *Caution Hikers — You are in mountain lion territory.* If I encountered a mountain lion, the sign suggested I was to pick up my child, so we looked like one giant person or shout really loud. Both of those things would definitely make a big difference. Especially since I didn't have a kid.

I followed a path that snaked around the mountain and gradually went up up up. Just like I kept saying to myself when my feet were getting damn tired along the way, I'm now saying to you — *We've come this far, are you willing to go a little further?*

See, I'm talking to you who might be reading this. It's taken me a few weeks to write this out, and it certainly shouldn't take that long. I kept writing surface stuff, just things that happened to me while I was on this trip. That's all fine, but I would be lying if I didn't say what was happening the entire time underneath.

As I get older and generally spend this after Christmas

holiday by myself, it gets increasingly harder. This one was especially difficult. I had always been okay by myself and often preferred it. I've been in relationships before, some quite substantial and important. None long-lasting. Perhaps I am just getting into an age where time no longer unfolds in front of me infinitely? I can see an endpoint, and to be honest, it would be nice to have someone at my side to walk towards it.

It just really got to me this time. I firmly believe that I don't deserve to be with anyone. Although I can understand that that statement is intellectually ridiculous, the feeling inside holds it to be an undeniable truth. It has been a pattern throughout my life and most of my relationships. It's a pattern I've been trying to understand better to perhaps break it. But time is getting short. There is an endpoint to all this, and it's coming faster than I imagined.

I'm at a point where I look back at all those experiences that were great but might've been made greater in being able to share them with someone. I have no one to blame except myself. I have a hard time detaching those parts of me that just doesn't make any sense anymore. Isn't there a point where you're supposed to be letting go of this stuff? Where you're able to cast all the unwanted parts of you away?

When I made it to the top of the mountain, I just sat under these giants trees that were lightly swaying in the wind. The sun crept between the trees. I just sat. Listened. I had stopped listening for an answer. I was not attacked by a mountain lion. I was trying to just do my best. I just listened to the trees, and the trees said: *Ah, maybe.*

I'M LEAVING IT

The sixth-grade teacher did not know she had a student with a prominent nose.

She was artistically inclined and attempted to inspire her young charges with her creativity. We were instructed to sit profile on a chair before an overhead projector (remember those?) as another student traced our head on to a piece of white paper taped to the sidewall.

When it was my turn, I sat down, and the light flashed on, causing an extreme silence, the only sound the hum of the overhead projector. You could hear the proverbial pin drop, and a feeling of shock and awe came over the surrounding students, for they had never truly been exposed to the surprisingly raw power of a very prominent nose. Of course, in those days, it was not referred to as prominent.

Big, yes.

Massive, maybe.

A Pinocchio-esque feature protruding from the centre of my face, this comparison somewhat fitting in a 'silver lining' kind of way as I wasn't even a good liar.

Although I didn't know it at the time, this was a defining moment in my life - the first time I was made aware of my big nose. As a child, you don't know that your ears are too small or your eyes are too big until someone else points it out. Those early years are perhaps the most contented you are with your looks because your physical attributes are in perfect proportion to the person in progress. I simply didn't know I had a big nose. Apparently, to find that out, all I needed was an art activity, an overhead projector, and a classroom of sixth graders.

We coloured and drew on our profiled heads, the idea to

make a design that fostered self-expression, to explore who you were as a sixth-grader. I coloured mine completely black. My grandiose claim, as I quickly realized everything would be eclipsed by the nose. We gathered around the bulletin board as the teacher hung the profiles and students played a guessing game to distinguish who was who. Instantly, a girl pointed at mine and said, "That's Paul." I already knew the answer, but I asked anyway, "How did you know?" She scoffed at my question and answered like it was stupid: "The nose." This was going to be a steep learning curve.

I have become proud of my very prominent nose. For a long time, my nose was a source of contention between it and the rest of my face. A repressed insecurity, hidden away except for the fact that it was on display every day. Literally, front and centre.

Some feedback I received was that my nose looked okay from the front, but once I turned in profile, it was just too much. This feedback came from a kid named Jesse, around the time of the overhead projector drawing, who took me around during recess asking everyone who they liked better, him or me. Since he threatened most of the kids to say they liked him better, he won the competition by a landslide. But for the next few years, I took Jesse's suggestion to heart.

The nose constantly leaks, especially in cold environments, the largeness leaving ample room for liquids and hardened asteroid-type mucus, and with constant worries that one of those asteroids were visible around the rim. I rarely blow my nose in public as it makes a horrible honking noise. I don't want to scare small children. It's not the kind of pleasant and amusing honking you might find used as sound effects in a cartoon. More like out of tune bagpipes being played by an elephant and filtered through a sped-up fog horn.

And hair.

As I grew older, there was a constant battle to keep ever-encroaching nose hair at bay. Gross. I can see my nose without a mirror, the outline filling about 15 to 20 percent of my lower peripheral vision. When I worked with young kids who looked up to me, literally, they confirmed my fears when they remarked, "You have a big nose." I laughed it off. One kid wanted to make sure I heard her, "No, seriously, I could get lost in there."

Around that time of the picture in profile was also when I started to figure skate. This did not do well for my already poor social status at school because, well, I did not know at the time, was not old enough to understand, that I lived in a society that was desperately holding on to notions of masculinity and femininity that taught boys to become men, that feelings and sensitivity were negative consequences of participating in a sport where I wore costumes and expressed myself physically through my body.

A society where when I taught kids skating, we still found it necessary to reward little boys with truck stickers and little girls with ballerina stickers. These kids projected their confusion when they pointed at me and said, "Earrings are for girls," or "Why are you wearing a pink shirt? Only girls wear pink." This antiquated top-down system was so firmly entrenched that when the former president of the United States dared to show emotion and wipe some tears away, his critics called him weak for it.

I might be reaching by comparing the plight of a boy figure skater to the president, but the thing is, people just needed to get over it. I really loved to skate, and I was mostly confused by the names that people called me. It wasn't until a few years ago when a teacher of mine sat me down and said that being sensitive and vulnerable were signs of strength, not weakness. To me, that guy was one of the manliest men

I know.

I was mostly a single skater but did pair skating for a few years. For those unfamiliar, pair skating is where a male and female skater perform lifts, jumps and spins together. And here is where figure skating, an object's moment of angular inertia (the object, in this case, being an elbow of a young girl), and the size of my nose came together in a perfect storm.

Now, when a figure skater is rotating in the air, they are going at speeds of upwards of 80 km/h, so when her elbow hit me, my nose snapped on impact. We were practicing a double split twist - where the man (in this case, me) throws the woman (in this case, her) into the air, she spins around twice, and he catches her, placing her on the ice. On the way down, I heard a pop, and my nose immediately started bleeding, as though someone had turned on a faucet. Pair skating is very dangerous, and we were taught to protect each other. If a lift was going down, our instinct was to get the person in the air back to the ice as quickly as possible. I must have gone into immediate shock because I remember putting her down, but don't remember any pain. Just all that blood. I remember standing there on the ice stunned. A parent of another skater leapt over the boards. I was rushed off the ice and to the hospital.

I sat in the emergency room with my parents for five hours. A broken nose looked bad, but it was not life-threatening. I sat quietly, trying to stop the bleeding while holding an ice pack to my face. I finally got in to see a doctor, who came in with a chart, looked at me and said, "Let's see. Your nose was straight at one point, right?" I was not in the mood for jokes. "Come back tomorrow, and we'll get that STRAIGHTENED out." A real comedian, this guy. My nose used to be straight, but now the bridge pointed to the side.

The next day, I returned to the hospital. I really hope they don't fix broken noses in this archaic way anymore. The surgeon dipped giant cotton balls into anesthesia and stuffed them all the way up my nasal cavity, a place that everyone - especially doctors - should know was exit only. I lay down, and they brought in two orderlies. The orderlies stood on either side of me, and each grabbed an arm at my shoulder. The doctor appeared over top of my face and put his fingers on my nose. And you know how they used to fix a broken nose?

They broke it back into place.

Slowly.

When it initially happened, it was fast, like a punch in the face. Or, in this case, an elbow to the face. The doctor proceeded to physically move my nose. And I started screaming. Whatever kind of painkiller they were using, it wasn't working. The orderlies were big men and I was a teenager, but they were still having a lot of trouble holding me down. The doctor would move my nose over a bit, stop, look at it. Pressed it over a little further, stopped again, looked at it. This seemed to go on for an eternity. Finally, he stepped back and said, "Looks good to me." They sent me home after putting a cast on my face that covered my nose, forehead, and cheeks.

I'd have to keep the cast on for three days. Three days of going to school wearing the equivalent of a neon sign on my face that read, "Look at the size of this nose." How was I going to explain this when I went to school? It wasn't something I could hide, there was a giant cast on my face. And it didn't happen in a cool way. A hat was the answer. A disguise that could shield me from ridicule.

I never blamed the split twist lift, I blamed the nose.

Back when I went to a Catholic school, we had to take

our hats off in class. Now I was in a public school, and this rule didn't apply, thankfully. Except in geography class. The teacher didn't have a cross hanging on the wall, but she insisted we took our hats off. I went early to the classroom and asked if I could have permission to keep my hat on - for obvious reasons. She graciously agreed and I took my seat in the back row, out of sight. At the beginning of class, she made an announcement, "Usually, I ask students to remove their hats, but I'm making an exception today with Paul." It's like I was back in front of that overhead projector.

I started thinking about famous noses, people who leveraged their most distinctive facial feature, and who didn't seem to be compromised by it. In fact, were known by it. The most famous of all, Cyrano de Bergerac, apparently fought 1000 duels over nasal insults. George C. Scott's nose played General Patton. Ringo Starr was a drummer in the band that redefined music. Chris Martin's nose didn't stop him from pretending he's Bono. Barbara Streisand was pressured at the beginning of her career to get plastic surgery, but stuck by her nose. Good decision, look what happened to Michael Jackson. But still, these famous noses only raised my hopes for a limited amount of time. Their noses a kind of amusing afterthought. In an interview with a late-night talk show director, it was revealed that Chad Kroeger's entourage instructed the crew to avoid filming the singer in profile due to his nose. This type of shame can only be matched by anyone caught in the audience at a Nickelback show. Ricky Gervais, unlike Kroeger, had David Bowie sing a song about his pug nose. He embraced his imperfection.

Still, there were no superheroes with a preternatural sense of smell, no crime fighters named Hound-dog that solved cases by smelling out their adversaries. After my formative years, I tended to look at people straight on, which had the curious side effect of them thinking I was very interested in what they said. Most of the time, I wasn't.

And then something else started happening. Although my nose remained large, the rest of my features seemed to fill out, and I didn't really notice it as much. I realized that no one really cared, it was I who attached such significance to the unusual size of my snout. It wasn't other people that needed to get over my nose, it was me who needed to live with it. Besides, it wasn't a piece of clothing or something detachable, although that would've been nice sometimes, it was a part of me.

One of the positive aspects of growing old is choosing my reactions, understanding that much of the baggage I brought to a situation was packed by me. Only through false blaming of how others perceived me and my own revelations surrounding the ability to realign my own internal perspective did I finally come around to accept much more than just my nose.

I stuck my nose into the minds of others, placed unfounded judgments in every word they spoke, believed everyone wanted only appropriately-sized noses with nostrils that did not resemble black holes from outer space. My nose has become my most distinguishable feature.

To paraphrase the sex advice columnist Dan Savage, every relationship fails until one doesn't. You learn something from each one. An ex of mine had a real thing for big noses - we even went to a show with her favourite comedian Demitri Martin. She loved my nose and couldn't get enough of me digging it into the base of her neck. She christened it 'prominent,' and I thought, what a perfect way to describe it. So like the boogers in my nose, but unlike that relationship, it stuck.

However, if there is one thing I've learned, it's that if I

ever break my nose again, no matter how bad it looks, I'm leaving it.

THE NUN

My mom told me I should go to visit The Nun. "Excuse me?" I said. I had become very interested in my father's family history. For some reason, that was never clear to me, my dad lost touch with most of his family after my grandmother - his mother - died.

The Nun was my dad's cousin, who lived in a convent for 60 years since she was 16 years old. My mom explained that she was somewhat of an informal historian of my dad's family.

I called The Nun and arranged a time to visit the convent, which was about a two-hour drive away. She insisted that I arrived for 10:00 am so we could attend mass in the adjoining church. Now, I'm not the most religious person. Actually, I'm not religious at all. I was more worried about her. I mean, she worked all her life to be closer to God, and now she was walking in with a heathen like me. Was I threatening her status? I quickly realized that it didn't work that way.

A tiny lady wearing a habit and flowing robes greeted me in the lobby. She whisked me right away to the church, which was filled with other nuns. Now, I don't know if you've heard, but not as many people are receiving the calling to be a nun. The convent was more of a retirement home.

After mass, we went to lunch. The word was out among the nuns: a young man was visiting. For most of that first visit, The Nun and I went from room to room where I moved furniture or got stuff off high shelves. In return, they each gave me chocolate for a job well done, and we sat and talked with them. I think The Nun liked bringing me around, explaining who I was to all the other nuns. I was a rock star in that convent.

We finally settled in her room, and The Nun unveiled this huge family tree that she worked on and updated for decades. She went through how my grandmother was one of eleven children, and I was so happy to hear that they were a bunch of weirdos. One of these great uncles worked as a tollbooth collector his entire life. When he died, they found decades worth of paintings he made that he didn't tell anyone about. The paintings were shown in galleries, and they were quite disturbing, all featuring, what I could only call, ghouls, in different scenarios. Ghouls eating lunch. Ghouls hanging out in a dungeon. Etc. Another uncle entered and exited his house only through the window. He had some phobia about doors.

And so on.

At certain times in the day, a bell would go off in the convent, signalling prayer time. Whenever the bell went off, The Nun stopped talking to me, looked up to the ceiling, had a silent conversation and turned back to me, said, "It's okay, I can skip prayers. Jesus wants me to keep talking to you."

She told me about a great uncle that had written a book. He fought in the First World War and had sent diary entries back home. This diary was found many years later and published as a book, describing his day-to-day activities as a soldier.

I left pretty overwhelmed with information. Every few months, I'd drive out to visit The Nun. We went to mass, ate lunch, got stuff off high shelves and sat down for our talk. The Nun was up to date on all the latest political stories and world events. She disliked Donald Trump even more than the pope seemed to.

After I returned from trips to places like China and Jordan, she wanted to know all about it. Her memory was sharp, and she was curious about other cultures and faiths. Although she referenced religion during our discussions, she respected my choices of faith or lack thereof.

When my mom called me to say The Nun had gone into the hospital, we made plans to visit one last time. The Nun could be stubborn and insisted that no one came to visit her. By the end of the day, my mom called me again, this time saying The Nun was moved to the hospice wing of the convent. My mom travelled on the train to my place, and we left in the early morning.

We made it to the convent, and the nurse explained to us that there was nothing more they could do for her. The Nun was sleeping, and it was the first time I had ever seen her without her habit. Another nun was sitting at her bedside. She smiled at us and said that she had arrived at the convent on the same day, 60 years ago.

When The Nun woke, she was so happy we had come. She had lost most of her eyesight a while back and liked to pull you in close when she talked to you. She took my mom's hand and said, "I told you not to come, but I am so glad you did." We sat at her bedside and talked and laughed and told stories.

For the entire day, there was a steady stream of nuns on rotation visiting with her. My mom and I decided that we had the chance to say goodbye to her, and although we were actual family, the family she should be with at these final moments were the nuns, whom she had lived with for 60 years.

When we said goodbye, she took my hand and pulled me in close. "Thank you," she said. "Thank you for all the times I got to live with our family again through you."

A few days later, my mom called me to let me know that The Nun had passed away. As I said earlier, I am not a religious person. But I got off the phone, got down on my knees and had a moment of silence in memory of my friend, The Nun.

BUTTERFLIES

I want to tell you about a friend of mine that passed away. He's one of the major reasons why I continue to keep writing. Our friendship lasted for a decade, and every moment spent with him was significant. Here are four examples from our time together.

Ten years ago, I had a nice corporate job with a great salary and was on track to keep moving up the ladder. Only one problem: I hated every minute of it. So, I quit. Quitting is highly underrated. I used my last paycheck to pay for a week-long intensive course at the Humber School for Writers, where I found myself in Wayson Choy's class. Before the course, I read all of Wayson's books - *The Jade Peony*, *All that Matters*, *Paper Shadows*, and *Not Yet*. Pretty great stuff. That week at Humber changed everything for me.

At the end of the week, we walked into the last class, and there were three things spread out on the desk in front of each of our spots. Wayson said, "These three items are all you need to be a writer. First, a pencil to write with. Second, an eraser to understand your mistakes and fix them." And it was even in the shape of a butterfly. "Third, and perhaps most important, a fancy pencil to dream with." And he walked around the room, stopping at each of us. He folded a piece of origami paper into a butterfly as he told us what he learned from us. "Paul," he said, "You have shown us a break in the clouds, now show us the entire blue sky." I mean, who talks like that? Wayson does.

After the course, we started writing letters to each other. Like, through the mail. I recommend writing people letters. When I found out Wayson passed away, I spent the afternoon reading through our correspondence and was able to hear his voice again.

Although he was retired from teaching, he took on one or two people per year to mentor, those that he felt were committed to writing in a deeper way. A year, two years went by as we worked on my writing together. I re-wrote another draft of my first book. I met Wayson at our usual café, and brought him the manuscript - I was so excited - and said, "Look, I re-wrote this using all the things you taught me." I don't remember exactly what he said, but it was something like - *Hmmm.* For the next six months, I submitted the manuscript to pretty much every literary agency and publishing company in - like - the world probably.

After those six months back in the cafe with Wayson, I explained how I had gotten all these rejections and how upsetting it was. He looked at me and said something like - *Hmmmm.* But then he said, "I knew when you showed me that manuscript six months ago that you were only going to get rejections." I said, "Oh, yeah, you could've told me that then." Because I can be a smartass sometimes. He continued, "I know you can write better. But you were so proud of your finished manuscript that you wouldn't have listened to me. Now I think you will listen, and I think you're ready to go deeper." I remember thinking at the time, *Oh, that's some Jedi mind trick shit right there.*

About two years after this, he decided that he couldn't teach me anything more. The power dynamic that exists in a mentorship can sometimes become unbalanced. He wasn't interested in that, and I respected and appreciated that he regarded me as an equal. We were just friends now, getting together almost every month or two. Wayson would call and dramatically announce, "Paul, we have much to discuss!" We'd usually meet at a café or diner and talk about life, death, faith, art, movies, and perhaps his favourite topic - gossiping about my love life.

Being the same age as my father, I often looked to him for advice or council. In the wake of my father's death, my mother needed a break, and I brought her to visit me for a few days. I set up a lunch with Wayson, and the three of us spent the afternoon together. Wayson was comfortable talking about death, and he reached across the table to take her hand, holding it tight. I was grateful that he was able to comfort her in a way that I couldn't.

"Paul, we have much to discuss!" Our lunches turned into all-day events. We'd start at our usual café and visit bookstores, second-hand clothing stores, and sometimes I'd just hang around to help him grocery shop. Because every moment with Wayson, no matter how small, was important. He taught me to pay attention to these small moments. Pay attention to the details, to the signs, pay attention to others, to the world, to your feelings, your instincts, your heart.

The last time I saw him was at a book launch a couple of months before he passed away. I was not in a good place in my life but was trying to get out more. I did not want to be at that book launch, but something told me to stick around for a bit more. Later in the evening, someone tapped me on the shoulder, I turned around, and there was Wayson. Noticeably weaker, but still smiling, he said, "Paul, we have much to discuss!" We made plans to get together, but it would not come to pass.

I'll end on a note he wrote to me on March 28th, 2014. This note was to me, but I switched out our names, as his words have more meaning than anything I could possibly end with: *Dear Wayson, After clinging so tightly to the self waiting inside you to skip, hop, jump, run, I hope you let go of this internal block and see yourself as others have come* to see you - brilliant, attractive, and sublime in all the ways that matter. My dear friend Wayson, I'm glad to hear that the riptide of currents in life holding you back has set you free.

Has set you free.

With love, Paul.

MEDITATIONS

David Bowie burst into the cabin. The hinged spring slapped the plywood door shut behind him. Bowie from his Ziggy Stardust phase. He swung around and with liquid fluidity, turned and pointed towards the window. The chicken wire covering the window lifted, and three giant spiders from Mars jumped inside. They danced around and with David Bowie.

I couldn't move, frozen on the hard bed.

The door swung open again, and a tiny car backed inside. Clowns dived out of the car windows, crowding the room further. They did flips and twists around and with David Bowie.

This dream was getting out of control. But it wasn't a dream.

I noticed a giant frog in the shadows. How could I miss this frog? He was the size of a bulldog. He just stared, the area under his chin expanding and contracting. I heard a cry of wolves in the distance. The dancing stopped. David Bowie, the spiders and the clowns jumped out through the window. The frog remained.

The door swung open again. A slimy hand grasped the door jam. An equally slimy foot stepped on the squeaky floorboards. The skinny sinuous pale body slithered across the room. The moon appeared from behind some clouds, illuminating the eyeless face and making the skin even paler. Its mouth displayed two rows of jagged teeth with red residue dripping off them. And it moved its long spidery fingers towards its face, covered where its eyes should be with the back of its hands and opened the palms. Eyeballs blinked at me. The frog's throat contracted. The pale man inched closer.

This dream was becoming a nightmare.

I was out in the woods, at a meditation retreat, a little more than halfway through my allotted ten days. Things most certainly have gone awry. It didn't help that right before I arrived, I watched the movie *Pan's Labyrinth*, and it scared the wits out of me. I should say that both the frog and the pale eyeless man made an appearance in the film. It was one thing to see them on a movie screen, but totally different from having them starring in my own dream, one that felt more real with each passing second.

I knew that this was a dream. At least, lying in bed, I kept telling myself that. But at the same time, the pale man kept moving closer, and the frog kept staring.

~

The bus ambled on down the dusty road. Living in Toronto, I forgot just how rural the surroundings quickly got once you left the outskirts of the city. We headed north, my directions vague at best. When I signed up for the ten-day Vipassana Meditation Retreat, I received an email that said to take the Barrie-Bradford Go bus and ask to be let off at a gas station outside Fennels Corner. Since cellular reception was weak in the area, I was instructed to make a collect call from a payphone located at the station. After approximately thirty minutes, a volunteer from the meditation centre would pick me up.

As my cell phone reception dwindled and the kilometres between houses grew, the bus pulled into the gas station. I could just say I was mistaken, that this wasn't my stop. But I came this far, literally in the middle of nowhere, and the few other people on the bus stared at me with tired eyes, waiting for me to make a decision.

Dust and dirt swirled around me in the wake of the bus. I watched it drive away, the road lonely and void of any other vehicles. Two women stood under the abandoned gas station awning, fanning themselves with magazines. Since there was no other reason for them to be there, I assumed they were waiting for the same ride. I approached and noticed that although one was quite a bit older than the other, they both shared similar features. After introducing myself, the mother and daughter faces lit up when I inquired about whether they were heading to the meditation centre.

"First time? Nervous?" The mother asked. They collectively giggled when I replied in the affirmative.

We waited in the hot sun. Cutting through the silence was a car engine. An old sky blue station wagon skidded into the gas station parking lot. A woman with long unkempt white hair jumped out, informing us that she was indeed from the meditation centre. Her large hands hefted our bags into the back of the station wagon. In the car, the three women conversed excitingly about the retreat. This was the mother-daughter team's third one.

The driver eyed me in the rearview mirror: "First time? You look nervous."

I was nervous, but why was everyone asking me this? Should I be more nervous? I was nervous, but for other reasons. The summer I went to the retreat, I found myself at a crossroads. Switching careers, looking at the world differently. Trying to figure some things out for myself. I was told I needed Vipassana.

In addition to the centre outside of Toronto, Vipassana can be found all over the world: ten in North America, three in Latin America, eight in Europe, seven in Australia and New Zealand, numerous sites in India and the Asia Pacific, and one in each of the Middle East and Africa. Vipassana is one of India's most ancient techniques of meditation, and since the time of Buddha, has been handed down by an unbroken chain of teachers. Considered a non-sectarian technique, the method has been practiced for more than 2500 years. During the course, I respected the secular approach, that is, you didn't have to be a Buddhist to gain benefits, and also how modern psychological concepts were incorporated into the teachings.

The ten-day retreat was completely free, including a place to sleep and meals. You basically went out to the woods and meditate for ten days in silence. Sounded cultish to me. Everything has a price. I wondered: what was the catch? I regarded myself as a cynical and stubborn person, two attributes that kept me from exploring a lot of things. But also kept me out of trouble. It seems everything has its cultish tendencies nowadays: religion, politics, corporations, yoga. I like my extracurricular activities with no strings attached. I did my research and couldn't find any cultish connections to Vipassana. I decided to sign up, my application was accepted, and that's how I found myself riding in a station wagon out to a mysterious campground with three women talking excitedly about the adventures of the mind.

We pulled into the meditation centre and stopped at a small check-in booth. A gentleman with a clipboard dutifully checked off our names and assigned us cabin numbers. The mother-daughter team was dropped off first, and they wished me good luck. They told me not to be nervous, but it was too late, as due in large part to their inquiries, I found myself quite nervous. Men and women were segregated during the retreat, and so we headed over to the other side of the camp.

There were three kinds of sleeping quarters. First, a new

addition to the camp was a building that had several small apartment-like accommodations. Second, individual cabins for single room occupants. Third, double cabins that were made from plywood, with glassless windows covered in chicken wire and which were only used in the summer due to the lack of insulation. I grabbed my bag and walked down a short dirt path to a semi-circle of the third kind of cabin. Found my number and pulled open the door and stepped inside. The door slammed shut behind me with a bang, the hinges fixed with tight springs. Two single beds sat at either end of the cabin. A sheet hung from a wire divided the two areas. Evidence of a roommate existed on the left side of the room. I dropped my bag on the dirty floor and sat on the hard bed.

My home for the next ten days. This was starting to feel like a bad idea.

Get your bearings, I thought. Outside, opposite my cabin was the washroom. Running alongside our cabins was a plastic fence that separated us from a group of three other small buildings that housed maintenance equipment. Trees flanked along the remaining border. Other people were milling about, and although I got a few polite nods, no one was talking, and there was a general sense of nervousness in the air. Perhaps I was not the only one.

I retraced my steps down the path and back to the dirt road. I came to a crossroads. Painted signs advertised one path towards the dining hall and another the meditation hall. I followed my stomach to the dining hall. People loaded supplies at the side of the building. I took a quick look inside and saw a standard mess hall with long tables and uncomfortable-looking chairs. I followed the path around the dining hall through the woods and came to a clearing in front of the meditation hall. A similar building but one that

I couldn't peek into. The buildings all seemed to share the same architect.

A loud gong rang. The man who checked us in banged on a metal gong hanging from the limb of a giant tree in the centre of the clearing. The gong signified that we were to meet in the dining hall.

People approached from all different paths, and we filed inside. The manager of the centre introduced herself and provided the lay of the land. The schedule consisted of getting up every day at 4:30 am to meditate for two hours. Break for breakfast and meditate some more. Break for lunch and meditate some more. Break for a late snack and meditate some more. You get the idea. At the end of each day, there was a lecture and in bed by 9:00 pm.

I am not a morning person. I don't want to talk to anyone in the morning, and no one wants to talk to me, at least not before I had a coffee. That's the other item the manager went over: *The Code of Discipline*.

From the website:

> Vipassana is not a rite or ritual based on blind faith, neither an intellectual nor a philosophical entertainment, not a rest, cure, a holiday, or an opportunity for socializing, not an escape from the trial and tribulations of everyday life. Vipassana is a technique that will eradicate suffering, a method of mental purification that allows one to face life's tensions and problems in a calm and balanced way, and an art of living that one can use to make positive contributions to society.

> The first rule of Vipassana is that you undertake the following five precepts for the duration of the course:

abstain from killing any being, abstain from stealing, abstain from all sexual activity, abstain from telling lies, and abstain from all intoxicants.

The second rule of Vipassana is for the student to declare themselves willing to comply fully and for the duration of the course with the teacher's guidance and instructions. Observe the discipline and meditate exactly as the teachers ask, without ignoring any part of the instructions, nor adding anything to them. This acceptance should be one of discrimination and understanding, not blind submission.

The third rule of Vipassana is the discontinuation of all forms of prayer, worship or religious ceremony, for example, fasting, burning incense, counting beads, reciting mantras, singing or dancing. All other meditation techniques and healing or spiritual practices should also be suspended. This is not to condemn any other technique or practice, but to give a fair trial to the technique of Vipassana in its purity.

The fourth rule of Vipassana is all students must observe Noble Silence from the beginning of the course until the morning of the last full day. Noble Silence means silence of body, speech and mind. Any form of communication with fellow students, whether by gestures, sign language, written notes, etc. is prohibited.

The fifth rule of Vipassana is the complete segregation of men and women. Couples, married or otherwise, should not contact each other in any way during the course.

The sixth rule of Vipassana is the suspension of physical yoga and other exercises during the course. Jogging is also not permitted. Students may exercise during rest periods by walking in the designated areas.

The seventh rule of Vipassana is dress should be simple, modest and comfortable. Tight, transparent, revealing, or otherwise striking clothing should not be worn. Sunbathing and partial nudity are not permitted. This is important to minimize distraction to others.

The eighth rule of Vipassana is students must remain within the course boundaries throughout the ten days. No outside communications is allowed before the course ends. This includes letters, phone calls and visitors. Cell phones, pagers and other electronic devices must be deposited with the management until the course ends. In case of an emergency, a friend or relative may contact management.

The ninth rule of Vipassana is the restriction of musical instruments, radios and reading or writing materials. Students should not distract themselves by taking notes. The restriction on reading and writing is to emphasize the strictly practical nature of this meditation.

In a sense, nothing, except ourselves. After a day, I understood. You didn't need any of this stuff at the centre. My reliance on external items such as cell phones and worrying about what I was going to wear quickly fell away.

I wanted to talk to someone about these rules. At the time, I felt they were a little excessive. That was one more item the manager went over: once we entered the meditation hall the first time, we were not allowed to talk until the end of the retreat. *Noble Silence.* Did I mention it was ten days long? Ten days with no talking. Not a word. As we made our way over to the meditation hall and moved into silence, I had a few final words that I spoke very quietly to myself.

Those words were: *Oh, shit. What have I gotten myself into?*

~

The bell rung in the farthest ether of my imagination. A dull, far off throbbing that searched for me and became louder with every clang. Still dark outside, freezing inside. I stumbled out of bed, wondering where I was and what happened to the sun. I looked through the chicken-wired window at a solitary person carrying a lantern and banging a bell. The vision slowly walked around the perimeter of the cabins, ringing the bell before each door.

Shivering, I put on almost every piece of clothing with me. A miscalculation on my part. I assumed that since it was the middle of summer, I didn't think I needed many clothes. But out here in the woods, I quickly realized that the warm mornings and sweltering afternoons translated into cold nights. Freezing cold. And obviously, little to no insulation was built into the cabins made of plywood and chicken wire. I certainly wouldn't have any trouble with Rule #7 regarding tight, transparent or revealing clothes.

As I walked along the path to the meditation hall, others joined me. We resembled the walking dead, zombies waking up from dreams, unable to speak, madly limping along half-asleep and still dreaming. My watch read 4:25 am. I can't remember ever waking up at this time. Staying up until this time, sure. Something inside me questioned the sanity of waking up voluntarily. *Everyone else was doing it*, I rationalized. *We can't all be collectively crazy, can we?*

Men and women entered the meditation hall on separate sides. We filed in silently and found our allotted mat and pillow. Luckily, mine was located at the rear of the room, which gave me the added ability to lean my back against the wall.

A weakness of mine that I was worried about was the inability to sit cross-legged for any length of time. Clearly, a problem when it comes to meditation. In the foyer, there was a large closet with extra pillows. Every time I walked in, I grabbed a new pillow. I started off sitting on one. Scored with two tiny pillows that I placed under each knee. Soon I sat on three pillows, had one under each knee and covered myself in a blanket I acquired the third day. The blanket especially came in handy at 4:30 in the morning when I didn't want anyone to see my face.

My body adapted quickly. Changed almost immediately. It was truly amazing to witness as my physical body completely streamlined into what my mind asked of it. *Body*, my mind said. *Look, we need to shut you down for a while. Run you on the backup generators while we charge the main battery. Don't worry, we'll run you at a functional level: eat, sleep and shit. That's all you need to be concerned about.*

The teachers entered the room, a man and woman, who I later learned were husband and wife. The man was tall, lanky and sported a Kramer-esque shock of hair that pointed straight up. I came to call him The Audio/Visual Guy, or A/V Guy for short. He never said a word, simply sat on his platform at the front of the class and pressed play on the CD player.

Through the speakers came singing, but not any type of singing I ever heard. Guttural, from the chest, phlegm-sounding. The singing, or chanting, were taken from the *Collections of Discipline and of Discourses* of the Pali canon, the language of the earliest Buddhist scriptures. This singing went on for a while, and a grave voice introduced the meditation technique. This was none other than S. N. Goenka, the latest in a lineage of teachers who preserved and spread this technique from generation to generation. He asked us to concentrate on the area between our nostrils and upper lip. Forget everything else. Just focus on this area, the breath that comes out of the nostrils and any sensations that occur.

And that was it.

I sat cross-legged, thinking about the area between my nostrils and upper lip. I thought about it, pondered it. Nothing happened. Sat there for two hours, bored out of my mind. You could feel the people around you. The man beside me was old and through a special request, had a chair to sit on. I wanted a chair. It didn't help that he uncontrollably kept farting for the rest of the week. Not smelly farts, but still. Eventually, the guttural singing started up again, and this sitting was over. No cosmic change yet.

The routine settled in. After this first meditation sitting, most people went to eat breakfast. I decided to return to my cabin and quickly shower while it wasn't busy. Made my way over to the dining hall and had my breakfast. Oatmeal, prunes and tea. Decaffeinated tea. I never ate prunes before this and have not had them since. Only old people enjoyed prunes. And did they enjoy them? I became addicted. Loved the prunes. I'm not big on small talk, but it was strange to be sitting with so many people with no one talking. We all just stared at our prunes.

During the breaks, I walked. Down the path that led to the main road, down the road towards the meditation hall, circle around back to my cabin area. Repeat. Five laps and change direction. Other walkers took to the paths. Since I couldn't speak to anyone, since they couldn't tell me about their lives, I started judging. A favourite past time of mine. I didn't think this was against the rules but could be classified as a negative sort of thought when attempting to have noble silence of the mind. The older guy who looked like he stepped out of a lawyer's office, the longhaired hippy, the ex-con. Judging other people based on their looks was wrong, but how else to get through the day?

The next sitting was mid-morning. After this, we broke for lunch. The food was incredible. Lunch was the big meal of the day. All vegetarian, all freshly made, with spices grown on the property. The volunteers in the kitchen were led by an intense-looking man who had to feed almost one hundred people with a kitchen the size of the one in my apartment. By the end of the ten days, we feasted on the likes of: miso soup, pasta, rice herbal bread, lots of salad, lots of tofu, vegetables, lentils, tempeh, chard, pickled beets, noodles, spinach curry, spinach fried rice, spinach by itself, beans, squash and fruit. Not my usual diet, but it's incredible what you are capable of eating when in the woods silently doing nothing. With a spread like that, I usually would stuff myself until I could no longer talk. But I took just enough to fill my gullet.

Walked some more and the afternoon sitting allowed us the option of being in the meditation hall or remaining in the cabin. I ended up falling asleep in my cabin.

There was no dinner, only afternoon tea and fruit. I

figured this would not be enough, but from the first day, I never felt hungry at night. The fruit and tea were more than enough. Sometimes I had an apple. Sometimes I had an orange. This was about the most difficult decision I had to make on a day-to-day basis.

More walking and another sitting in the early evening. At the end of the night, a television rolled into the meditation hall. The A/V guy pushed play, and we watched and listened to a lecture from Goenka. A man with a strong presence (even through the TV) and with a happy disposition, he laughed a lot and told stories. He always began the lecture by saying, "Day two is over, eight more days left." Thanks, like we needed reminding. After the lectures, bedtime.

All told, we meditated for ten hours in total per day. Sleep did not come easy, the body might have been functioning at a bare minimum, but the mind was fully awake. Even if I wasn't aware of it yet, things were changing, realigning, restructuring.

~

Sleep, wake, meditate, walk, eat, shit. Repeat. The first three days were somewhat repetitive. That was the idea. On the fourth day, everything changed.

The two concepts that stick with me to this day and which I still attempt to figure out is impermanence and equanimity. Goenka discussed impermanence in many of his discourses:

When one experiences personally the reality of one's own impermanence, only then does one start to come out of misery. If one tries to possess and hold on to something that is changing beyond one's control, then one is bound to create misery for oneself. Commonly, one identifies suffering with unpleasant sensory experiences. Still, pleasant ones can equally be causes of misery, if one develops an attachment to them because they are equally impermanent. Attachment to what is ephemeral is certain to result in suffering.

In a sense, he was talking about the art of dying, that many of these things we deem essential as we live are impermanent, including our physical body. The cynical side of me understands that this is a difficult concept to fully appreciate. On an intellectual level, I have thought that we must look at the unpleasant things in life, try to work them out, and by exploring these ugly aspects of human nature, come to some kind of greater understanding. On a practical level, this is damn hard. Goenka continued:

This is not a path of pessimism. The technique teaches us to accept the bitter truth of suffering, but it also shows the way out of suffering. For this reason, it is a path of optimism, combined with realism. Each person has to work to liberate himself or herself. This is not a dogma to be accepted on faith, nor a philosophy to be accepted intellectually. You have to investigate yourself to discover the truth. Accept it as valid only when you experience it. Hearing about truth is essential, but it must lead to actual practice.

Equanimity stems from being aware of how you are functioning internally. During the ten days, we were learning to sit quietly and listen to the inner workings of our bodies and minds, attempting to create some sense of balance between all the elements of who we are and how this translates into our interactions with our internal and external worlds. Goenka continued:

> Whenever a difficult situation arises in life, one who
> has learned to observe sensations will not fall into
> blind reaction. Instead, he will wait a few moments,
> remaining aware of sensations and also equanimous,
> and then will make a decision and choose a course of
> action. Such an action is certain to be positive because
> it proceeds from a balanced mind; it will be a creative
> action, helpful to oneself and others. Gradually, as one
> learns to observe the phenomenon of mind and matter
> within, one comes out of reactions, because one comes
> out of ignorance. The habit pattern of reaction is based
> on ignorance. Someone who has never observed reality
> within does not know what is happening deep inside,
> does not know how he reacts with craving or aversion,
> generating tensions that make him miserable.

Hammering woke me. Ordinarily, this kind of thing annoyed me. I started to awake out of sleep before the bell sounded. I stepped outside and found the source of the hammering. On the other side of a fence separating our cabins from the maintenance area, a man worked away laying some plywood. From what I could tell, he was building another storage cabin. He hammered away, either not aware or not caring that it was 4:30 am in the morning.

Zombies walked to the meditation hall. Every morning we looked less and less like zombies. My imagination might have been playing tricks, but my fellow meditators seemed fresher and livelier. The morning meditation went off as usual. At breakfast, the prunes were especially delightful.

Our next sitting started a new phase. After singing, Goenka announced that this began the Sittings of Strong

Determination. A slight change in technique brought on internal chaos that not all of us could handle. He referred to this change as us performing surgery on ourselves.

According to Goenka, from the lecture on day four:

Saṅkhāra, a mental reaction, is a seed that is made from every moment. A reaction with likes or dislikes, cravings or aversion. There are reactions that make a very light impression and are eradicated almost immediately, those that make a slightly deeper impression and are eradicated after a little time, and those that make a very deep impression and take a very long time to be eradicated. At the end of a day, if one tries to remember all the Saṅkhāra that one has generated, one will be able to recall only the one or two that made the deepest impression during the day. And like it or not, at the end of life, whatever Saṅkhāra has made the strongest impression is bound to come up in the mind; and the next life will begin with a mind of the same nature, having the same qualities of sweetness or bitterness. We create our own future by our own actions. Vipassana teaches the art of dying: how to die peacefully, harmoniously. And one learns the art of dying by learning the art of living: how to become master of the present moment, how not to generate Saṅkhāra at this moment, how to live a happy life here and now. If the present is good, one need not worry about the future, which is merely a product of the present and therefore bound to be good.

With our minds, we scanned from the top of the head down to our toes. Find the pesky Saṅkhāra, puncture it and allow it to be released from us.

I finally understood why we focused on the area between our upper lip and nostrils. The idea was to sharpen our minds and concentrate on one area, so when we moved throughout our body, we could zero in and move about internally. During the Sitting of Strong Determination, we were not allowed to move or open our eyes, no matter how uncomfortable.

As soon as we started, someone from the front screamed for help. My eyes remained closed. Some rumblings about. My eyes remained closed. I sensed the person was escorted from the meditation hall. My eyes remained closed but desperately wanted to open. My open anguish was apparent, so the external person asking for help fell so far outside of my body that he ceased to exist.

My cynicism stopped being a problem. There was no spiritual awakening, no religious epiphany. But what did happen was my body exploded in images. A movie played in front of my closed eyes, with main characters looming large and supporting actors receding. No longer in a meditation hall somewhere out in the woods. Nowhere, really. Floated, flew, it felt as though someone dropped a giant vat of jello on my body, but I didn't mind, even if I didn't like jello.

And the singing returned, and the first Sitting of Strong Determination finished. I left in a daze, a haze over my mind, my eyes seeing the trees and the path and my cabin and my bed, but seeing them in a somewhat confusing way. During the optional mid-day meditation, which I skipped, I stood watching the man hammering away. This wasn't meditating, but sort of. He had the base of the cabin finished, four walls waited for a roof. It was hot, sweat dripped from his brow.

More surgery the next day. During the afternoon sitting, we were allowed to approach the A/V Guy in groups of three and ask any questions or field any concerns. I had no questions or concerns, I just wanted to remember what it was like to talk. We got one question each, and the A/V Guy's response was always the same, "Just follow the technique." I attempted to throw in a follow-up question, but he wouldn't have it. The idea of not talking was so we could truly focus on ourselves. Keep things internal. Silence and the relatively simple techniques created a powerful paradigm that unclogged the mind and allowed things to flow freely. I think they offered you the chance to ask questions to make sure everyone was doing okay mentally.

Shingles were being hammered into place on the roof of the new cabin. Later in the day, he added a coat of red paint that matched the rest of the cabins. Three days this man worked on that cabin and now it was finished. He could step back and see the results of his efforts. Watching this man build the cabin had a finality to it. When do you stop renovating your brain?

"You have completed Day Seven," Goenka said. "Three more days to go." Again, thanks for reminding us. Day 7? Felt more like Day 700. This was around the time I felt things slightly slipping. Although the technique was meant to sharpen your mind, make things more transparent, I felt foggier. The fog thickened.

Sleeping was almost entirely out of the picture. I lay awake, sensitive to every little noise, creak, broken branch, slight gust of wind, footsteps, rustle of leaves. The wolves sounded their cry every night and circled my cabin. I was afraid to look through the chicken-wire covered windows out of fear sharp claws would rip my face off. This was no way to live. And in my mind, counter-intuitive to the reasons of me being at this retreat. Wasn't this supposed to relax me? Clear my mind? Allow me ten days away from the clutter and noise of the city?

That's when the door of the cabin slammed open, and David Bowie appeared. Followed by the spiders and clowns. The giant frog in the shadows. The eyeless man with the chiselled teeth. I cried out - screw the rules. Or I might have just cried out in my dream. I couldn't even ask my roommate for help. But was this a dream, or was this really happening? As the pale man stepped closer, I followed the advice of Indiana Jones at the end of *Raiders of the Lost Ark*: I closed my eyes. This would make everything go away.

The next thing I remembered was the wake-up bell. Convinced it was all a dream, I went about my morning routine. As everyone ate breakfast, I headed towards the shower. I turned the water on but didn't notice at first the frog sitting in the corner of the shower stall. Although it was a normal-sized frog, I nearly jumped. It just stared at me the entire time until I finished. This could have been a coincidence, after all, we are out in the woods, and there was a stream running beside our cabins. A frog could have easily found its way in here. But this was my rational brain talking, a part of my mind that was slowly losing grip. At least there were no clowns, no Ziggy Stardust, no spiders and especially no pale man.

~

My space in the meditation hall was becoming a pillow mountain. The days ran together, my mind in a state of mushy contemplation. This was never going to end, the rest of my life was going to be spent inside the routine.

On the eighth day, everything broke apart. During the Sitting of Strong Determination, my will snapped. Again, nothing resembling a giant fireball of epiphanic symphonies, just a slow popping of intimate somethings. Little did I know that change was happening incrementally. A simple idea emerged, a concept that should have been obvious in my outside life, but for some reason, went unseen. Everyone and I mean everyone in my life, no matter if it was merely a walk-on part, appeared. They all crowded into the meditation hall, and we just stood there looking at each other.

It was at this moment that I realized I was loved.

Even now, I hesitantly write this word loved, but I find no other way to put it.

Everyone stared, said nothing (we couldn't – Noble Silence), but the most important people in my life looked on with love in their eyes. It was also at this moment when all the tension and angst left my body, my shoulders slumped from the release. I just let go, let it all pour out of me. Tears flowed, silent tears that I didn't wipe, that I let come. For perhaps the first time in my life, I didn't care what anyone else thought, because I was loved.

The man finished painting a second coat on the cabin. On the second to last day, he loaded it with tools, work clothes and a riding lawnmower. The storage cabin was new but fit in with the rest. There was nothing left to do but make use of it.

We piled into the meditation hall for our last sitting. At the end of the sitting, Goenka lifted our Noble Silence and once out of the meditation hall, we were allowed to talk. As we filtered out of the hall, no one said a word. We were in shock. What do we have to say? We just smiled. When I finally did talk to my roommate, my throat was hoarse, my voice crackling. It sounded funny to me.

My judgments about most of the people around me were wrong. I learned that my roommate came from a hard-lined Catholic upbringing. He always believed in what the church had to say about life and where you go when you die, but these beliefs have been firmly challenged after this week. All this talk of stored Saṅkhāra and impermanence and how our life was one long lineage of individual moments that evolved and continued seemed to make sense to him. Although he had more questions than answers, he seemed at peace with this.

At lunch, I spoke with the middle-aged corporate lawyer look alike. He told me a long story about how he was CEO of a large charity. He had a wife, children, a nice salary, big house, fancy car. It was never enough, and he started taking drugs, which led to an addiction to crack. Lost his wife, children, salary, house, car. Just out of rehab a few months previously, these ten days were hard, but he made it.

The old farting man told me another long story. About his hard life of poverty, about how he always shut people out. He started studying martial arts, and the instructor told him, "Your body is impenetrable, you need Vipassana." He signed up.

When we burst into the dining hall for lunch, there was a party waiting for us. The tone was completely different. Everyone that helped in the kitchen met us with smiles. Before, it felt like they were ignoring us, but I assumed this was part of their instructions. They were genuinely happy for us because they knew the feeling. They all had gone through the course and knew what was on the other side. My cynical outlook took another hit. No one tried to solicit anything, no one tried to sell us anything. In the corner of the room, a small desk was set up, and we could give a donation if we felt compelled. That was all they asked from us. They just really wanted to help people.

I returned to the city. Every telephone wire buzzed. Every leaf rustled. The voices in the crowd all separated. I sensed every detail, every noise was specific.

Equanimity, impermanence.

My awareness was sharp, but I was not overloaded. I heard every detail but didn't feel burdened. And in all that noise, amidst all the clutter, there was silence. The silence separated from the noise. The silence spoke. The silence said I was loved.

PART FOUR:
NOWHERE TO GO BUT UP

ACT ONE: THE ACCIDENT

Sitting in the cab of the tow truck, I took a drag of a cigarette and coughed.

"Married?" The tow truck driver asked.

The only strength I had left was to shake my head.

"Divorced?" He guessed.

Another shake.

"Kids?"

My voice barely audible, I let out a coarse, "No."

I tried the cigarette again. Coughed again. This time more of a hacking fit. The cigarette was supposed to be calming my nerves.

"What do you do?" I wished he'd be quiet. I wished I had enough strength to tell him to shut up. I barely had enough strength in my normal life, let alone at this moment in time.

"I work in television," which I usually tell people I don't want to talk to. For some reason, it always made an impression and bought me enough time to move on.

We sat in the cab of the tow truck on the shoulder of a major highway, and there was no escaping.

"Remember the *Hulk* movie?" He asked.

"Which one?" At least I was thinking straight. This was a legitimate question.

"Not the old stuff. And not that artsy one. And not those crappy *Avenger* movies. The one with, what's his name, the guy from that movie where they beat the hell out of each other? The movie with that other guy? There were the two of them, and they beat each other up. You know. "

"*Fight Club*."

"Right. The guy from *Fight Club*, not the one guy, the other guy-"

"Edward Norton," I chimed in with a sigh.

"Yeah, that guy. They filmed that *Hulk* movie around here. I helped with some of the driving. Did you work on that *Hulk* movie?"

"No."

"Did you see it?"

"No."

~

Funny how quickly your life could change in a matter of seconds. One second I was driving on a ramp to merge with a major highway. A few seconds later, I stood at the side of the road, my car much smaller than it had been.

Early in the morning, still dark, I was driving to the airport for a work trip. Never was a fan of early flights, but at least getting to the airport was less of a pain. Making good time, I drove along one highway and took an exit to transition to another highway to the airport.

Usually, I'm pretty good about keeping an eye on the area around me. Changed lanes into the left side to make it easier to merge. My guess was the truck in the right lane wanted over too, but there'd be plenty of room once we were on the highway.

The truck driver didn't check his mirrors.

It happened so fast.

The truck clipped the side of my car. With that touch, the world went into a clichéd sense of slow motion. A gentle nudge, barely felt, like if you were in bumper cars and someone touched you as they moved along. That nudge, along with the highway speed we were travelling, sent my car spinning across three lanes of traffic.

Spun around once.

Luckily it was morning, and there was not a lot of traffic. Spun around twice.

The steering wheel was no longer in my control.

Spun around a third time.

No traffic except for that large truck heading right for me.

When I saw the truck, I heard someone screaming. It took a moment to realize that the person screaming was me.

The exact order might not be correct, but it happened something like this. As I spun around one last time, the truck hit me full speed from behind. The airbag was triggered, and since I was screaming out the side window looking at the truck, punched me on the right side of my head, making my neck snap backwards. The force of the truck hitting me from behind caused the car, completely out of my control, to slam into the guardrail.

And I stepped right out of the car.

Stunned, I stared at what was left of it. The hood and the trunk were completely destroyed. Basically, the entire vehicle was smashed except for the front seats. The truck that initially clipped my car stopped in front, and the second truck stopped behind.

The driver from the first truck arrived first. He looked in my car, looked at me and said, "You hit me."

I couldn't speak yet.

"I saw it," he continued. "You hit me first."

Then he returned to his truck and sped away.

The first on the scene wasn't the police or an ambulance, it was the tow truck. They ride along the highways with radios equipped to hear police reports of accidents. The tow truck driver would be the most compassionate person throughout this process.

He looked at the car, and said, "Don't worry, insurance will cover it. You been drinking?"

My brains had been scrambled, I was almost killed, and he's now implying I was drinking at five in the morning?

All I could do was shake my head. Even that hurt.

The ambulance was the second to arrive, but they didn't stay long. Did more of a drive-by. They slowed down, and a paramedic stuck his head out the window, surveyed the scene. "Everyone looks alright here," he said. They drove off.

The tow truck driver led me to his cab, and we sat in silence until he said, "We've got to wait for the cops. Mind if I smoke?" I shook my head. He took a cigarette from his pack and offered me one. My hand shook as I tried to light it. He took the lighter from me and lit it himself.

Then the bit about the *Hulk* movie.

The policeman arrived, and the first thing he asked was the drinking question again, but phrased it differently: "Have you been out all night drinking?" Listen, I understand that they were asking these questions because people must still drink and drive a lot. However, unless you're obviously drunk, couldn't we lay off the victim-blaming? He asked me a few basic questions about what happened, and he went to check the car. He was gone for what seemed like a long time.

"Okay," he said. "I see marks along the side of your car that are consistent with your story. You said the other truck driver fled. Did you remember what kind of truck it was?"

I shook my head, "He said it was my fault."

"Yeah, you were in shock. He probably stopped to make sure no one was dead."

"Comforting."

"You'd be surprised how many people hit and run."

"You're not going to find him?"

"Chances are unlikely. But, I'm putting into the report that you are not at fault."

The truck driver yelped. "That means the insurance

company is on your side!"

The policeman gave me a copy of the report and left. We hitched my car and drove to the garage. The tow truck driver gave me the license plates from my car and explained that a rental vehicle arranged through my insurance company was on the way. He gave me some water and told me to sit down in the lounge area.

I knew a friend of mine got up very early in the morning, and I needed to connect with someone. I sent her a message asking if she was awake. She responded right away, and I told her I was in an accident. She asked if I wanted to talk about it or did I want a distraction? Distraction. She went into detail about the television show she watched last night.

The phone call to my mom was when I broke down. After getting into an accident and calling a loved one at an unusual hour, never start with, "The first thing is: I'm okay." Something in her voice broke open the floodgates of all the emotions I had stuffed down.

A mess, I went into the washroom and steadied myself. I avoided the mirror because I didn't want to see my eyes. Didn't want to see in my reflection how my life had changed in the span of a few minutes.

My rental car arrived. Not a car, but a huge SUV. The kind of SUV that I scoffed at when people drove these tanks around downtown. The car rental guy shrugged and said, "It's all we had left."

After pulling out of the parking lot, I stopped a block later. This was insane. I just got hit by two trucks on the highway, and now I was given a rental car and expected to drive home alone. I steadied myself some more and drove through rush hour in the most cautious way possible. Commuters were not happy with me or my giant SUV.

At home, all I wanted to do was go to sleep. After being on

the phone for too long with the insurance company, I finally made it upstairs to my bed.

Something from the deep recess of my brain screamed, GET UP! My eyes snapped open, and I remembered a First Aid course I took years ago. Most of the information was forgotten except for one instruction. If you suspect someone of having a concussion, DON'T LET THEM FALL ASLEEP.

Even though the paramedics thought everyone at the scene looked okay, I really should get checked out by a doctor. Up out of bed and walked down the street to a walk-in clinic. Something must have been wrong because I was whisked in almost right away.

"So, you were just in a car accident?" The doctor asked.

Nodded.

"This sounded like a very serious accident."

Nodded.

"Did an ambulance come by?"

Nodded.

"They didn't take you to a hospital?"

Her questions were getting difficult to answer, but I continued best I could. Finally, she asked, "Do you always talk like this?"

"Like what?" I asked.

"You're slurring, searching for words and seem confused at times."

What was she talking about? I wasn't slurring or searching or confused.

"You've suffered a major concussion, so that is normal. You also experienced whiplash, pulled your lower back and sprained your wrist. Are you married?"

Why did people keep asking me that?

"You can sleep, but you need someone to wake you up every few hours."

I limped home and crawled into bed. I told a few friends that I would send them a message every couple of hours. If they didn't hear from me, they were to presume I was dead. This joke didn't go over so well.

~

Over the next few weeks, I didn't do much of anything. Concussions are still very much a mystery, and people suffer all kinds of symptoms. Mine consisted of the inability to parse out information. When we go out into the world, there are a million little pieces of information flying at us. In one day, the average person encounters over 100,000 bits of digital words. That's a lot of words. So, your brain is parsing out what is important and what's not. For example, if I was sitting in a restaurant, there's the clatter of utensils, music playing, chatter from other tables, and so on. All that information is still there, but my brain tunes it out so I can focus on the person sitting with me at my table.

No parsing for me. When I would go outside with all that information coming at me, I'd get two hours tops, and be exhausted. Some people with concussions suffer from light dysphoria - having to wear sunglasses inside and even at night and limited exposure to computer screens and smartphones. This wasn't such a problem for me, so I sat around watching a lot of television.

I became obsessed with private detective shows. Which, in this day and age of television, there was no shortage of. I started noticing some patterns in these shows. Most of them were about middle-aged white men suffering from a mid-life crisis. Sometimes the storyline incorporated an alcohol or drug problem, but not always. Most of the time, they were a big city cop who had just moved to a small town. They were the best detective the city had seen, but they crossed a line, got into trouble and usually ended up depressed. The small town an attempt to run from their problems. But their problems seemed to find them everywhere. As it often played out, murders or other violent crimes started right around the time the big city cop arrived. Of course, these crimes reminded him of his past mistakes. Small towns are strange places. Weird sex and violence seemed rampant. The locals were suspicious of the big city cop, and they should be as he uncovers all their dirty laundry. Also, cell reception sucks out in the sticks.

As I sat on my couch watching these depressive shows, I was unknowingly - or more accurately, knowingly - falling into my own depression. It didn't help to expose myself to these dark and violent shows deep into the night.

I developed an unhealthy relationship with food. Instead of stuffing my gullet to help my brain, I was feeding it a constant stream of comfort food. After all, I was recovering from a major accident, so I decided to go easy on myself. But there was going easy and there was being irresponsible. It feels a little strange to be talking about my eating compulsion - I'm not what you would refer to as overweight. However, I'll slam just about anything into my mouth, that is, anything with meat and salt and that is generally terrible for me. Processed food? It's easier to make. Chips? Why, yes. At midnight? Why not? All this sitting around and eating was starting to show on my waistline. When I gained weight, it all went to my belly, which was extending. This extending caused me to stand differently with my back at an angle. This angle started causing extreme back pain. This pain kept me on the couch.

I was getting caught in a loop - sit around, eat, sit around more, eat - repeat. Each day I had less motivation to do anything. Physiotherapy sessions were ongoing, and acupuncture needles were stuck all along my body. My physiotherapist kept repeating that I needed to eat better and even try some exercise. I nodded a lot and said, yeah yeah yeah.

Physical exhaustion was also due to a lack of sleep. Whenever I closed my eyes, I was back in that car, spinning around. The truck. The screaming. Immediately after an experience such as a car accident, the brain formed memories attached to the trauma and liked to replay them for you at odd times. Within five hours, those memories are pretty much fixed. Or, took a lot of time to untangle. I became scared of silence and darkness.

Another symptom I had was the stuttering and searching for words. You know that feeling when you can see the word in your head, you know what you want to say, but you just can't remember? That kept happening all the time.

A few weeks after the accident, I scheduled an interview for my podcast. The guest didn't know about the accident, and I was scared to death that I wouldn't be able to talk properly. I wanted to get back to my life. When recording, I wore headphones, and so my voice got piped into my ears exactly as it sounded. Then a most bizarre thing happened: as soon as I hit record and the interview started, the stutter and searching for words went away. I sounded like my old self. I remembered how, when some people with a stutter sang along to music, it took their mind off their voice, and the stutter disappeared.

I tried one other experiment. A month after the accident, I had a show where I was to stand up in front of an audience and present a story. I have a certain base level of anxiety over speaking in front of people anyway, so the stutter did nothing but add to it. The same thing happened - no stutter, no searching for words. Enough distractions were going on in my head during these times and not enough room for anything else.

I couldn't always be either in a state of performing in front of people or doing podcast interviews. Very slowly, the stuttering and searching for words went away. Slowly.

At my second appointment with a neurologist, he told me I checked out. No MRI because I was getting better with each appointment. He wasn't worried, so neither was I. He told me to take fish oil and meditate.

Two deeper problems were triggered after this last visit to the neurologist. First, he told me I could drink alcohol - in moderation. Second, the voice in my head came back with a vengeance.

ACT TWO: HEARING VOICES

"You dumbass. Stupid. Idiot. Who in the hell do you think you are? How many times do I have to call you an idiot until you finally see that you are worthless and full of shit? What's funny is that everyone around you can see it. But you? You seem to have blinders on to the level that others put up with you.

"Stupid, dumb, asshole.

"Look, we've gone over just how ridiculous all this is. That client, they are going to fire you. In fact, they are going to ask for all the money they've already paid you. You're going to go bankrupt. Remember that homeless guy sitting on the street who asked you for change on your way home? Yeah, that's going to be you. First, you'll be fired, then you'll have to return all the money anyone has ever given you, then you'll lose your house and all this crap you call your belongings. How do people become homeless? Not all of them are as big a mess up as you, but you'll be joining them soon. Pick the one stupid outfit you have, pack a goddamn bag and say goodbye to all the people in your life. Dumbass."

That's me talking to myself. Everyone has an internal voice, this is how mine talks to me. It likes to provide daily updates on how I'm screwing up. This is not an outside person that I am speaking to, it's a style of dialogue that I've cultivated over many years since I was young. For about as long as I could remember.

The voice gets right to the point.

Sure, there are new age, self-helpy terms like negative self-talk and stuff like that. I get it, but what doesn't help is identifying it in such a way that makes it angry and uncontrollable and refers to me as gullible, ridiculous and forever a prisoner. The voice didn't just come into being, it was created over time, and over time, it turned on me.

The voice definitely existed when I came into existence, it lay dormant inside my own mind. If I was to think very hard, I'd say the first time I came across it occurred during my figure skating days. As previously mentioned, I was a competitive figure skater, an athlete who trained every day.

Analyzing this nowadays, I believe the voice wanted to keep me in a box. It really came on strong when I attempted to step out of my comfort zone. It would be right there to slam me back down.

"You're going to come last in that competition next week. You suck. Look at who you're competing against - you are by far the worst skater. You should give up now and save you and everyone around you the trouble of having to be kind and say things like, 'Well, you gave it your best shot.' Sure, it might be your best shot, but your best shot sucks."

Stuff like that.

I believed this voice in my head because deep down, I knew that it was me talking. I believed these things about myself. I had no choice, really. If you encounter a bully who, every time he sees you, tells you that you suck, you can just try to avoid this person. The voice is carried around with you, around every corner, no matter how deeply you attempt to silence it, it only comes back stronger and with resolve.

When I would be all dressed up in my nice figure skating costumes, and step on the ice to my starting position, my brain would be firing on all cylinders. An argument raging inside my head. The voice screaming at me to just give up, while I tried pushing myself through all the motions. But usually, the voice won out. It became an ongoing feedback loop. The voice convinced me I'd do bad, so I'd do bad, re-affirming that the voice told the truth.

In a way, I started to believe that the voice was trying to protect me from myself. Instead of living the kind of life that I could be, the voice was showing me the reality of what my life is and will continue to be.

When I got into university and started exploring different avenues outside of being a competitive athlete, the voice was there to tell me I was full of crap. I took writing classes (Don't even think of reading this drivel out loud to the rest of these people - you're wasting everyone's time). I started making my own films (You need to burn the film that was used to make this).

Most importantly, I started making new friends. The voice was quick to point out that these were friendships based on proximity. The only reason most of these people talked to me was that they wanted something from me. And that thing wasn't friendship, it was a recognition that I knew how to work and make things. Other people could participate and then take credit, using them to further their own lives, agendas and careers.

Cynical? Maybe. Bitter? Not yet.

The films and the writing did suck, I won't deny that. Isn't that what everyone thinks of their work from years ago? Or is that the voice still lurking in the dark recesses of my mind? That the perspective of my personal history is so tainted and fixed by the voice that I will never be able to see things simply as they are? Maybe, maybe not.

After university, I started working at a small production company where I learned almost everything I know about storytelling through visual mediums. Still, if anything went wrong on a project, the voice was there to lay blame at my doorstep. Film and television are collaborative arts that involve many different people through many stages of production. Didn't matter, even though I usually performed my duties at the highest level, working through nights, pushing myself, I believed that it was never enough.

Years went by, and the voice realized its true strength. At points of physical and mental exhaustion, the voice could stroll into a situation and completely take control over my mind. I was still me, I still functioned, interacted with people, worked. It was like going into a fog where the real me seemed very far away, so far that I watched myself from outside of myself. No one noticed, no one could tell.

I remember very clearly a moment during a relationship I was in at the time. We often worked side-by-side at my apartment. This was the first time someone recognized that I was not myself, that the voice had taken over. I was working very hard on my own personal creative projects, and something did not come through that I had focused on for a long time. I lay on my bed, staring blank-eyed at the wall. She was reading at my desk, looked over and was shocked by what she saw. What she saw was not me. She crawled into bed with me and just held me. That was exactly what I needed - for someone to just know that the voice had taken over. Just touch me, bring me back.

A project I was working on at the office beat me. After months of working around the clock, the project was finished. At that moment of release, of physical and mental exhaustion, the voice meandered in and took over. Took over for years, really.

Burnt out, I left that job that had been a big part of my life for years. After working for so long, I wanted to do something that held very little responsibility and had a small time commitment. I went back to my athletic roots and started teaching little kids how to skate.

The voice was a constant presence at the time. Moving into my 30s, most people around me were doing adult things like getting married and having children. This was not on my radar as the voice continually let me know I was a worthless person who no one considered lovable.

If I did manage to go out on a date, the internal dialogue was laser-sharp, pointing out every single detail that I was getting wrong.

Example:

We would be out at a coffee shop, something simple and with zero pressure. Didn't matter. Inside, my brain would be on fire: "Why did you say that? If she could, she'd walk out immediately. She hates you. She can't wait to get out of here. You are an idiot who will always be alone."

And so on.

Basically, in most interactions, two narratives were going on. The one that the world saw, a somewhat seemingly well-adjusted individual who, although might be living a lonely kind of life, was sort of endearing with a self-deprecating sense of humour. The second, deeper one, was hyper-aware of every word, motion and action happening around him. It was like when they started releasing DVDs with audio commentary by the filmmakers, except the person doing my audio commentary was the voice, who essentially was my shadow side. Try it sometime, with everything that happens to you, automatically bring it to the most negative result possible. It's neither pleasant nor helpful.

During this time, I moved a bit out of the city. What I didn't realize was happening was that I had given myself over to the voice. Not entirely, not yet. But a piece of me. By moving out of the city, I isolated myself from friends and others. I lived a quiet life, one where I didn't do much. The less I did, the less things the voice had to comment on. By not doing things or talking to people, the voice was a little quieter.

This was no way to live. After years like this, I rarely heard the voice because I rarely did anything.

After a certain amount of internal silence, some opportunities presented themselves to me. A gnawing feeling started poking me, this feeling like I had been a failure. No, this wasn't the voice talking, this was me. Me, coming up for air, looking around and thinking, "What the hell are you doing with your life?"

Out of the blue, I got a television job offer to work at the Olympics in Russia. Two things happened in Russia: I learned to control things with my mind, and I killed and buried the voice beside the Black Sea.

During the entire process of getting a Russian visa and preparing for this trip, even though I felt I was not qualified for this job, the voice was relatively silent. Still, a bit shook from years of having given over to this voice, I was once again stepping out of my comfort zone. With each day of silence, I gained more and more confidence.

The plane ride was long. We landed in Moscow and were led through the airport to another waiting area for the next ten hours. I didn't know anyone on the production team, most of them had worked together for years. I was the new person, and they were understandably wary of me. I was unproven, it was unsure if I was up for the job. What they didn't know was that I had covered most of this ground myself. At least we were on the same page.

In Sochi, the palm trees were a strange backdrop for a winter Olympics. I learned later that some of those palm trees weren't real, and had people in them spying on us. Take that as a truth if you'd like.

The compound we were staying in was literally that - a compound complete with barbed wire. The reason this was in Sochi was that we were trapped. The Black Sea on one side, mountains on the other. There really was nowhere to go. Our visas were our accreditation, and our accreditation only got us specifically into two places: where we slept and where we worked.

We arrived by the busload and checked in at the same time. When it came to my turn, I had to sign some papers, but they were all out of forms. The hotel manager said, "We have someone running through the night with a new printer. They shall arrive here soon." Once the person came with the printer, a young female volunteer grabbed a handful of keys and told me to follow her. Construction on most buildings was not yet completed, so some rooms would be unsuitable. The lock on the first room didn't work. She walked into the second room and said, "You don't want to stay there." The fifth room seemed all intact, the only problem being that there was no showerhead. Exhausted, I just let her know that this would be fine, and we would sort out the showerhead later.

The internet was spotty in general, but a mistake was made in my favour. Someone placed a modem in my room, providing high-speed internet. I figured if I just didn't tell anyone about it, no one would notice. A trade-off for lack of a showerhead.

In the morning, I did a belly dance to wash up. The water worked, but it came out of a pipe about chest high. Curiously, the shower was up a step but had no ledge to stop the water from basically flooding the bathroom floor. It took me a few times before I figured out the best way to be efficient without soaking the entire bathroom.

Although there were buses that drove us to the area where we worked, I walked almost every day. Sochi was basically a resort town, and even in February, the temperature floated in the mid-20s, hence the palm trees. It was a nice walk, a path led through a field and along the Black Sea. There were several checkpoints to get through each day. The guards were not messing around, and I was told later that these were Russian army. As a local said, "Look them in the eyes, their eyes are blank."

On that first day of work, at our first meeting, where I had to make a strong first impression, that was when the voice emerged. Naive me, thinking that it had been somewhat contained. Stupid, idiotic me thinking that after travelling across the world to Russia, that the voice would have left me alone. It waited, bought its time until I was here, trapped in another country, where I had to put myself so far out of my comfort zone on all levels - professionally and personally. It came down on me like a blunt instrument.

We had a brief meeting and then a rehearsal. The rehearsal was a disaster, and the voice told me that they were going to send me home. Afterwards, we all mulled about outside our television truck, the executives in one group, the crew in another. All of them stopped talking whenever I walked by. I felt the voice smiling and thinking, "Who the hell do you think you are?"

On my walk home on that first day, I needed to make some decisions. The voice and I had a screaming match beside the Black Sea. I was here; other people paid for me to be in Russia, to be a professional, and they didn't have time for me to screw around. I compromised with the voice, I asked that it could say whatever it wanted, but to get it all out now. If it was out to completely destroy me, Russia was the perfect place. It could end me professionally, and I could never fully recover personally. But if it ended me and fully won, then what would it do? The compromise I made was an understanding that the voice could never fully win, it constantly just brought me to the brink. If it succeeded, there would be no reason for it to exist.

That night, I came up with a plan. To get through the next month, knowing that the voice was back, I had to learn how to navigate around it. Not work together, that's a bit of a stretch. I had to be aware of it, allow it to have its say, but be able to keep going and get done what I needed to do.

My role was director in live television. Live, which meant there was no room for mistakes. During a ten-hour day, decisions were made every few seconds, and once they were made, there was no fixing them. I had to make sure I was right. On my second day, I called a meeting with my production team. With the voice screaming in my head, I went through the process I had created and made sure that we all knew what we were doing. Well, what everyone else was doing. Me? I had no idea.

We started the live broadcast, and things started to run smoothly. The approach I figured out was this: the negative thoughts that the voice screamed at me, I turned into a physical thing. A small red ball, to be exact. Whenever the voice yelled at me or laughed at a decision or call I made, I simply turned it into a small red ball, and with my hand, threw it over my shoulder. Sure, the place was filling up with red balls, but since they were imaginary, that was okay. Day after day, I let the voice tell me all of the bad things I was doing, let it snarl and gnash its teeth. I packed these statements into little red balls and threw them over my shoulder.

Being tense ten hours a day every day for a month takes a toll. On my last day, the last show, everything over and the job successful, I went for one final walk along the Black Sea. When I walked far enough, I found an empty field and jumped off the boardwalk, my feet squishing into the mud.

A single tree stood in the middle of the field. When I

reached the tree, I collapsed to my knees and started digging with my hands into the dirt. I took the tiny red balls and placed them into the deep hole, covering it back up with mud. As I walked away, the voice was still loud but muffled. As I got farther and farther, the voice became a distant memory.

For the first time in years, on the entire trip home from Sochi to Moscow to Toronto, a silence descended on me like I hadn't felt in, well, ever.

Little did I know, the voice was not finished with me yet.

ACT THREE: SELF-MEDICATION

I was a good teenager, partying was not even on the map. Being a competitive athlete, it just wasn't a consideration. There was no worry about being invited to parties with kids from school. Male figure skaters do not really fit in well with high school.

Sure, I was called the usual things, but it was more confusing than anything else. I really did love to skate, although it might be more due to it being an individual sport as opposed to a team sport. I mean, who wants to be a part of a team? And have everyone disappointed in you when you inevitably mess up? As an individual figure skater, the failures fell squarely on my own shoulders. Or, at least they did in my own mind.

Plus, the main perk was my straightness in a sport full of girls. Trust me, enough people thought I was gay and felt compelled to communicate to me their hunch, that I did think about this a lot. Maybe I was gay? I would be okay with that if it was the case - it seemed to be other people that had the real problem. Besides, who wanted to be on a hockey team with a bunch of stinky boys? At the figure skating arena, I was a superstar.

There might not have been a lot of school parties, but once we hit driving age, skating parties happened all the time. Still, nothing interfered with my training. I was never really a heavy drinker, just something appealed to me about being able to shut off my very active mind. What I didn't know was that at the time, I was trying to quiet the voice, which started rumbling away and commenting on my life.

During my first year at university, I remained a competitive athlete, but it didn't last long. There was too much happening around me. People seemed to like me in university, you weren't forced to be friends with people due solely to proximity. I found like-minded people who, most importantly, were cool. I was most definitely not cool, so this attention was surprising. Really, when I looked back at it now, only one cool person liked me, but that was enough to warrant invitations to parties. I was now on the list.

Yes, drugs were around, but that was one addiction that never really stuck. Pot only enhanced the voice, removed any shackles on it. Inside my own head, I sounded stupid, and when I spoke, even more stupid. Mushrooms made me think I had reached a different level of consciousness, the kind that many young people experience in university. Ecstasy happened precisely once, and for those few hours, the world finally made sense to me. Still, the next few days of withdrawal were so terrifying and depressing that I never touched it again.

Alcohol was my drug of choice. And I enjoyed every minute of it, even the hangovers. The hangovers were me punishing myself. For what, I still don't really know.

As I graduated from university, I turned into a workaholic, a kind of -holic that still haunts me. But, I worked all the time spinning my wheels and didn't really get much further than from where I started. I wonder why?

I started working at a production company, and there were many late nights and long hours. Just to complicate things, I had my own production company where I made my own films. Often, I'd be at the office either finishing a work project or something of mine, my boss being generous enough to let me use all the equipment.

Work hard, play hard.

Finishing work was being let out of a cage. The alcohol consumption was justified here because I worked so hard.

Really, deep down, I knew that I was way in over my head at work and with my own projects. The voice made sure to let me know all of this. But, I managed to control and create some kind of balance. I managed, treading water to such a functional capacity that when I finally sunk, it was such a shock that I wouldn't recover for years.

A period of forced self-exile pulled me out of the need for balance. Moving out of the city, it was no longer convenient to go out for a night of drinking. Sure, I'd have the odd couple of beers at home, but mostly, I just read and wrote and worked. This was the point where the voice became somewhat smug, having thought it won the war. It was relatively quiet, and so the need to self-medicate not necessary.

After working at the Olympics in Russia, I came out of the self-exile and made my move back downtown, closer to new friends, experiences and, of course, bars. My creative projects were not over, being reignited and with it, the voice realizing it had to become strong, had to become heard again. It was an arms race to the bottom.

What happened next was a conflation of several small incremental movements, movements that I barely noticed. At the time, I could talk myself into almost any kind of behaviour. A large part of my life became managing my vices with the sole goal of no one finding out just how messed up I had become.

The car accident happened, which caused the concussion, and strict instructions from the neurologist not to consume alcohol. Since my health was a priority for the first time in direct relation to alcohol, I found other things to do with my time. Food was a big one. My primary source of comfort food was the trifecta: bowl of instant ramen noodles, bag of chips and a large peanut butter cup chocolate bar. I didn't eat this every night, but it was definitely my fall back when

I wasn't feeling so great, which was a lot. I opted for food I thought made me feel better, rather than food that would actually make me healthier. It's obvious to state now, but it's really important what you put into your body. Just let me own that stupid statement, it takes me a bit longer to get to logical conclusions.

The weight gained right in my stomach, causing it to extend like I was pregnant. As stated in Act One, this caused me to walk and stand differently, which caused lower back pain, which caused me to sit around even more, which caused me to watch more television, which caused me to eat more. And did you know, eating a lot of bad food adds to depression? Right, something else that took me a while to figure out.

The concussion healing nicely, the neurologist, without me prompting, approved the consumption of alcohol. I stopped at the beer store on my way home. After all that time sitting around, the voice had gotten very loud, really come around to letting me know about how I should have died in that car crash. Whenever someone referred to how lucky I was, the voice was there in the background, reminding me that there will be a next time, and I won't be so lucky. I started with a beer every other night or so. Just enough to dull the voice a little bit. And it worked. One beer every other day became a beer every night.

As I recovered from the concussion, my father died. At the time, I thought I dealt with it maturely and pretty much went back to work. These things have a way of creeping up on you.

An interesting side note is that during my time with my dad in the hospice, the voice was gone like it was never even there. Maybe it was scared of health-related environments, scared that it could be externally detected? Maybe it was that when in the hospice, my reason for being was so clear, so undeniable, that it did not know how to react, how to criticize, draw negative conclusions to my actions?

Now, I am not categorically blaming any of these things for what happened. It was a terrible combination of my own devices, and my internal problems being exacerbated by these external forces. I'm not a victim of anything or any person, I am a victim of myself. I created a need to self-medicate because I didn't know how to deal with myself, let alone anything majorly stressful. The voice just became too strong, it overtook me in a most quieted way. It actually didn't have to do anything, after a lifetime of listening to it, trying to manage it, it created the ideal situation: I was destroying myself from the inside out, a broken person who had no self-control and needed only the slightest nudge over the cliff.

There were very clear rules. I never drank before 8:00 pm, but by 8:01 pm, the sound of a beer opening echoed in my apartment. Another rule was that my place could not reveal this problem. Beer cans were disposed of immediately in order to not pile up. After eating some crappy food, usually take out, I'd sit at my desk in front of the computer screen. Just sit and watch a terrible action movie or several episodes of my private detective shows. Staying up late became the norm, convincing myself that I was just a 'night person,' thinking, no believing, that this was how I processed things. My way was to stay up late, turn my thoughts over and over to understand them. Often, I slept on my small two-seater couch to make it easier to get up in the morning. The rationale being that the more uncomfortable I was, the easier it would be to wake myself up. Along with being a 'night person,' I was not a 'morning person' or so had affixed this to my personality.

That was it, my life converged into simply sitting around trying to kill that part of me that still existed. I convinced myself that this was just my life now. Self-medicating in this way does not rob you of a life, it could provide a very active life, but in the end, it does rob you of a soul. Mine was being sucked out of me at an alarming rate.

When I would go out, I'd leave early, stating my old age and need to get up in the morning. The truth was that if the activity didn't involve alcohol, I excused myself to go to my empty home and crack one open from my stash. No one noticed, I became good at hiding it. I was quickly becoming invisible, to other people and most damaging, to myself. The isolation from friends and family became evident to no one, not even myself. I played people off each other. I was always an odd person, something my friends and family were aware of, so it didn't seem so strange. I could go from one person to another, disappear for a few days, and no one noticed. From what I could tell, I was fooling everyone (which I was most likely not) and what a terrible way to treat my friends.

All I had to do was reach out and tell people, talk to someone, anyone. Shame over my behaviour during this time and my problems provoked silence and the inability to communicate. Shame is highly underrated and can cause more harm than I imagined. The voice started in on this, convincing me that no one wanted to hear from me, that they were embarrassed to be my friend, would be shocked over my lack of self-control. The voice silenced me, it won. I didn't recognize it at the time, but when I look back, my life truly hung in the balance. It would have been very easy just to completely give in, give over to the path I was setting out for myself.

I always viewed drugs like alcohol as a way to explore my subconscious, in a way, believed that my mind was too active, and I needed to shut down certain parts to turn on those areas that I wanted to access. At different points in my life, alcohol might have helped me in social situations. Being a shy person, my anxiety could get the best of me and alcohol helped curb that. But when does a line get crossed? When does it become necessary to function? During those few months, I was simply becoming numb. My brain became mushy, which I was able to chalk up to the concussion. No one noticed. My reasoning and reality devolved into not understanding my direction. I didn't notice. All motivation was lost, there was no sense in doing anything, but not in some grand way, just a general feeling of disgust with myself and a light hum of disappointment. No one noticed. When you're generally already a misanthrope, hiding a new and profound sense of your worthlessness is easy. I dwelled in this cynicism, sunk deeper into a well where the only person that was there were myself and the voice, who continually, in a light whisper, let me know exactly where I was heading.

I knew how I was going to die. My apartment is a loft that has two levels with a steep curved staircase. I was convinced that one night, one too many beers to realize I need to be careful on the stairs, stairs that are wood and could be slippery when wearing socks, I'd rush down, slipping and breaking my neck below. My phone out of reach, I would only be found when someone tried to get a hold of me and finally got the building manager to enter the apartment, finding me bloated and broken. Certainly not the most glamorous way to die, but inevitable.

People often talk about hitting bottom. My bottom wasn't exciting, but I am thankful it was not falling down to the bottom of the steps. I just got sick of myself, sick of the voice, too tired and understood that I couldn't continue on like this; I had to make a choice.

There was something that gnawed away at me. When in the hospice with my dad, I sat with him overnight. He was sedated but still conscious. He communicated with me by the squeezing of a hand. One squeeze for yes, two for no. I sat holding his hand, an intimacy that often didn't happen between us. I was having a conversation with him, and I asked, "Do you think I could be a better person?" One squeeze.

During the following months, that squeeze stuck in my head. At first, I interpreted it as him being disappointed, that he felt I was not the person he hoped I could be. But one winter night, in a slight haze of beer and bad food, I was back in the hospice room holding my dad's hand. Somehow I cut through my mushy mind, found an ounce of strength to shut down the voice for a minute and realized that he wasn't disappointed in me, discovered that he knew I was a good person, it was just I had the potential to be even better. Now, you could say this interpretation was reaching, and that the squeeze of my hand could mean just about anything. But, I needed something to hold on to, something that lived within me to counter the narrative that the voice had set up for me.

As the voice returned, I realized something else. For as long as I could remember, the voice was inside my head but felt like it was someone commenting on me. Maybe this seems obvious, but I had a thought, just something simple that I remembered thinking long ago - the voice was me. And if that voice was me, then I was the one in control, not the voice. The voice was an extension of me. Therefore, I was in charge, not it. And if I was in control of the voice, then there was no reason to try to silence it. The voice was a part of me that I was attempting to shut down when really, I could change the script. I could change the words that the voice spoke to me. There was something behind the voice that I was not dealing with which were bi-products of a deeper problem. Maybe my father was right? Maybe I had the potential to be a better person?

ACT FOUR: THE HEIST

That went on for a while, this self-medicating. I wasn't getting flat out drunk every night, but it was becoming a consistent activity. I'd be fine during the day, then passing a beer store, I'd think - I'm stressed, tomorrow I'll stop. But, this can only go on for so long before you have to make a choice. My life can continue on this trajectory for, well, ever. Something has to give. This is a plateau because the level of alcohol consumption and sedentary living was becoming such an integral part of my lifestyle that there was very little room to move, either forwards or backwards.

Or, I could try and change. Yes, people are trying to change all the time, I hesitate to use the word evolve, but that's the ideal thing, right? Don't we want to get better as people? I'm too busy oppressing myself. The voice spewed hatred and violence all focused solely on one person: me. The voice screamed and shouted and let me know how much of an idiot I was at any given time, in any situation.

Have you ever been exhausted with yourself? Emotionally, my soul felt like it was slowly getting sucked out of me. I was drowning very slowly, and the voice laughed at my inability to swim. I wanted to choose to get better, but my resolve to even get started was eroding daily. In very little time, my sense of self might be gone forever.

Alarm bells should have been going off, but when you are pushing yourself down, you're holding your own head down under the water, disabling your own ability to breathe, complete shutdown and apathy become normalized.

Everything becomes too hard. Eating right? I didn't know how to cook and didn't have the energy to figure out how. Exercise? As a former competitive athlete, I knew that it took a while to get back into shape. That period where you were getting into shape could be difficult and seem like it was taking forever. I had a few starts and stops over the last few years. The figure I remembered was for every one week of sitting around, you were putting yourself three weeks behind. So, basically, I was years behind. Just thinking about it made me less motivated.

When I started writing this book, I knew I wanted to reserve the last part for this story about the voice and self-medicating. Of course, I avoided it for a while and put it off for as long as possible, mainly because I hate these kinds of stories. No, I don't hate them, I like them when they're honest. The stories around these subjects usually revolved around some type of lightning bolt moment where everything changes for that person. Does that actually happen? Maybe it happens to other people? Maybe they are honest with their stories, but my point is we have the tendency to tie these things up into a neat narrative. "My father died, and that's when I knew I had to stop drinking." Etc. Sure, I had moments like these, but really, when my dad was dying, I was kind of focused on him dying. I'm a selfish person, but not that selfish.

Let's take other people out of it, this isn't about them. For me, it was a series of incremental moments. I'm a bit loathe to admit that it was a self-help book that made me make the first decision that led to other choices. Suffice to say, I'm not too impressed with self-help books most of the time. This author was a vegan triathlete, and I heard him on a podcast. He talked about being a former competitive swimmer turned successful lawyer/alcoholic. After he recovered, he went on to change his diet and started racing in triathlons. You probably see where this is going. The book was pretty much the usual recovery narrative, but then at the end, there was an appendix that outlined how the author changed his diet. Where he was different from others was that he explained that it was not as difficult as you might think.

My diet consisted of a lot of meat. I tried one other time a while back to go vegetarian and did it very poorly. Changing my entire diet was a drastic mistake, and my body, probably going through some kind of withdrawal, totally crashed out after only a few days. This time, I wanted it to stick, and so just started with that simple idea - it's not as difficult as you think.

I did need to make a lot of changes in my life. What I needed was time, I needed to reboot my system. So, essentially, I started from scratch, removed myself from most commitments and began by making one decision at a time. The first place I wanted to start with was what I put into my body.

The first decision I made was simple: for the next week, I wouldn't eat any beef. A week went by, and I didn't put many thoughts towards consuming beef in any way. After a few weeks with no beef, I made the decision to not eat any pork. This seemed to lead naturally into not eating any chicken. From there, I became much more conscious and aware of what I was eating, even started buying cookbooks and making my own food. After a certain amount of time, it just seemed integrated into my routine, and I didn't have to think about it. My clarity, focus and energy all went through the roof, and I thought: who knew that what you put into your body was so important. I am the king of obvious statements.

Something else I hate about self-help books or recovery stories is the tendency to think the way you improved your life is what everyone should be doing. Bull shit. I'm much better with other people's stories when they let me choose how to engage with them. You never know what little piece of information will be a catalyst for change.

What I'm outlining is a way that I've gotten better, and there's still lots of work to do. As my diet got better, I focused on my body. Worked through those first few weeks of pain, of moving my body, stretching parts that hadn't been stretched in years. It was like there was scar tissue covering every joint in my body, and I had to break it all apart to move freely again. I approached this with the same mentality as the diet: one step at a time. I just set out wanting to do a few things each week, pushing myself a little bit further each time.

My body returned to normal faster than anticipated. My mind was an entirely different matter. During most of that downward spiral year, I spent it writing a different manuscript than this one. Entirely fictional, it was about a man who suffers a psychotic break, recovers in a hospital, escapes from the hospital and tries to build a new life halfway across the world. Of course, his old habits creep up on him and are more challenging to get away from than he had thought. There is a lot of dialogue between the main character and an internal voice that mocks and oppresses him. He can't get away from it, even at that place, halfway across the world. Wherever you go, there you are.

I desperately wanted to write about this idea of an internal negative voice. Still, that fictional novel never got at what I wanted it to be. Why was I scared to write about this directly? Because I'd have to admit to certain things in my life that no one knows about. Secrets.

The voice didn't one day stop talking or go away. The voice is still there, talking right now, in fact. Just as a check-in, it is saying, "This part of the story really sucks. No one will read it. I mean, who wants to read about your idiotic perspectives on health and well being? Dumbass."

The more you use the internet, the more it learns about you, and in turn, it curates and presents the world that makes sense to your preferences. The more I'm learning about the voice, the more I'm learning how to control and curate what it says about me. Listen to it, be aware of it, but also understand that it is me talking, so there is a way to navigate around it.

The voice is a bully. The more you push back against a bully, the harder they return the blows. You can outsmart a bully because chances are, they are not that intelligent. I hate bullies and have been dealing with them my entire life. Most of the time, they win, but how can I lose against this one in my head?

A way I learned to deal with the bully in my head was I made it feel safe, made it felt like it was winning. That was all it really wanted was to win. If you made it feel like it was winning, then it might back off enough to provide you with some breathing room. Then, you might not have a lot of time, but you might have just enough.

The heist started with the microbes. I learned about microbes when looking into patterns of behaviour through the lens of neuroscience. Millions of microbes cover our body and similar to how the internet uses algorithms to determine our preferences; we teach our microbes what kind of food we crave. I liked this concept, but at the same time found it depressing - how can we change if these millions of microbes had predetermined our wants and desires? But wait, we can retrain the microbes to want and desire completely different things. So, with each part of my diet that I changed and each time I exercised, I focused on those microbes and pushed them to want something else - to desire all that was good for me. I did this under the radar of the voice, very quietly and incrementally, one microbe at a time. The microbes took a while.

There was one shot at the heist. I was stealing back my mind from the voice. Stealing it back while it still had some value to it. As I got better, there were some days where the voice came on strong, beating me down, making sure I didn't get too big of an ego with all my pretentious dieting and exercise. I let it talk. "Idiot - who do you think you are with your kale and quinoa?" Keep talking, I thought.

I pretended that I was just doing a yoga class, yoga being something I returned to in my effort to exercise more. My plan was to use the 45-minute class as a distraction that the voice could focus on. As I progressed through the yoga class, the voice was on a bit of a tear, doing a running commentary the entire time.

Meanwhile, I snuck into the building of my mind through a basement vent. After popping the vent screen, I set my watch alarm to 45 minutes - the length of the yoga class. Pushed the up button for the elevator. The elevators were grounded as the voice had disengaged all electronic devices in the building until this particular yoga-tirade was over. Bursting through the door to the stairwell, I had to climb 40 stories in short order. Good thing I had gotten myself back into shape, otherwise, I don't know how I would have made it up all those flights.

I opened the door to the penthouse very quickly because I knew that the voice had protected the area with heat and vision sensors. The floor was dark and only had emergency lighting. I crawled under and stepped over all the lasers that would trigger the alarm. When I reached the other side, I came to a keypad and fingerprint scanner. I guessed the easiest number I could think of - bullies are not very smart, remember - and placed my hand on the scanner. Of course, it matched my fingers because technically, this all happened inside my head. As the giant air-sealed door opened, sitting in a glass case in the middle of the empty room was my mind. The alarm on my watch went off, indicating I had mere minutes before the voice realized someone had snuck around all its defences. I only had one choice: I pushed over the glass case holding my mind, smashing it to the ground.

Before I had time to pick it up, a shrieking alarm echoed against the walls. The large door started shutting, aiming to seal anyone who dared enter inside. I grabbed my mind and ran towards the door, slipping through right before it slammed shut. No longer caring about the heat and light sensors, I ran through all the lasers, setting off more alarms, triggering a cloud of gas that was released through the vents. I took a breath of air into my lungs and lunged out of the room into the stairwell. When I started running down the stairs, the stairs flipped over, creating a smooth slide-like contraption all the way down the 40 floors. At first, I thought this was an easy way back down to the basement until I realized there was probably one more trap at the bottom. As my momentum grew and I went faster and faster down, I could see the bottom. The floor had turned into a giant trap door. The speed was simply too great, and there was nothing to hold on to, no railing, nothing. I slipped off the slide and into the blackness, still grasping my mind in my right hand.

As I fell through the darkness, I slowed down and wondered where this was going to lead. It was as though the darkness went on forever, and I couldn't make out where I would ever land. Finally, I realized what I needed to do. I took my mind, which I was still holding on to, and shoved it into my ear. At this moment, I was thrusted back into my apartment where I finished up my yoga class. I stopped what I was doing and I listened for the voice. It was still faint, still there as a presence, but it was dull. There wasn't such a thrust behind it. Ever since then, it was like the volume has been turned down, taking away some power, restoring that power back to me.

I've never been diagnosed with depression or with any other form of mental illness. I don't claim to compare my experiences with those that are more severe and serious. But how can we get into a war of who has a more serious disease? What does this achieve? This was difficult and painful for me, this is an ongoing battle. At times I'm winning, and most of the time, I'm losing. Slowly, over time, I'm winning more and more.

None of the things that I have written about in the last four acts are to blame in this narrowly missed downfall. The point of all this was to recognize that with a few incremental movements, we can really slip into another place that is not easy to return from. In the same way, we can get out of these terrible situations in the same incremental way.

What I don't want to say is that by doing these things, I got better and now you can too! Bull shit. The point is, we're all alone in this, in the end. That's not me being cynical or reactionary. Yes, we can get help. Yes, we can read other people's stories. Something fundamental has to change internally to allow us to make structural changes. After almost a full vegetarian year, I went back to eating meat. I still drink alcohol. I have a much better understanding of how to control these things. And what could happen if they get out of control. I don't regard this as a failure, I'm trying to be easier on myself.

In my situation, my problems were small, minute experiences that led me to hate myself and never want to admit that I didn't need to hate myself. Isn't that a bizarre statement to make about yourself?

I think about how I have treated my mind, it getting scrambled in that car crash, torturing it through self-medication, abusing it with inactivity. My mind is how I make a living, it's the most appealing thing about me. Why would I not be better to it? How could I be better to it?

Maybe my dad was right? Maybe I could be a better person? You have to start somewhere, and it's a series of small incremental movements to something better. I know above I said we're all alone, but in a way, there are lots of us out there, all of us silently broken in ways we cannot express or are afraid of expressing. We have a shared connection and perhaps some of us are lucky enough to speak from the darkness, break the silence, pat hands on shoulders and get a little better each day together. It's examining all of the millions of microbes in my body, looking at each one and trying to change and form them into something new. A new person, a new body, a new personality, someone who is both the exact same person while at the same time becoming an entirely new entity. The same, but different. Me, but not me. You, but not you.

A better person.

ACKNOWLEDGEMENTS

Some of these stories originated at the live event, Stories We Don't Tell. My most profound appreciation goes to all the storytellers, audience members, and hosts that have enabled us to keep this going for over five years. Extra special thanks to my colleague, co-conspirator, and dear friend, Stefan Hostetter.

There was a story in this collection about my time with Wayson Choy. Even though he taught me what to do with my words, I still can't seem to express enough how much he is missed.

My name is on the front of the book, but another person made it look great. Big thanks to Ellen Yu for lending her incredible talents and ideas to come up with the brilliant cover.

To my family, I appreciate all of your amazing support. Maybe my nephews will be able to read my books when they're older. My father's presence is throughout this book, and I think about him every day. Of course, my mom has been and is still my biggest cheerleader.

ABOUT THE AUTHOR

Paul Dore is the author of *Dreams of Being a Kiwi* and *The Walking Man*, which the Quill & Quire called, "A globetrotting tale that imagines new ways to get at what's really going on." He lives in Toronto with his aloe plants Peter and Mary.

To learn more, visit pauldore.com.

FURTHER READING

If you enjoyed *I'm Leaving It*, look for other books by Paul Dore wherever you buy online. To learn more about Paul's work - podcasts, live events, books - visit his website pauldore.com.

The Walking Man begins in the deserts of Jordan and explores a year in the life of the main character - someone very similar to the author - and his attempts to make sense of a tumultuous year. Based on many of the author's experiences, *The Walking Man* mixes reality and fiction in a tale of heartbreak, friendship, and personal history that uses walking to thread it all together. Whether he is tripping through a blackout in downtown Toronto, stumbling into a massive war re-enactment, or outwitting the law while speed-walking beside his 93-year-old scooter-riding confidant, Mary, the Walking Man eventually makes his way, on foot, all the way from Toronto to Niagara Falls in his quest to find the truth.

Dreams of Being a Kiwi: Our hero hit rock bottom long ago. Suffering from a debilitating mental illness, he finds himself tucked away in a hospital. Despair kicks in and he sees no way out of the darkness. Then a kiwi comes along and brings hope into his existence. He soon fills his days and nights with dreams of travelling across the world to a new and peaceful life. Dreams are different from reality. He can only plan his plane tickets, ferry rides, and cross-country trips so far. When he finally takes the leap towards his goal, he finds adventure, love, and battles with the greatest foe of all: himself.

Stories We Don't Tell (co-curator) is a live storytelling event held in living rooms across Toronto. For five years, hosts have warmly welcomed us and our audiences into their home where a lineup of performers share personal stories about their lives. Some stories are sad, or a little weird, or intimate, and others funny. This anthology includes 61 stories that were all told in front of a live audience at one of our shows. The authors of these stories have generously contributed these pieces of their lives to be included in this book. Each story created a memorable moment in front of a roomful of people. Moving through this anthology is an experience where these many moments complement and reflect each other, contradict and draw parallels, have profound wisdom and absurdity. Welcome to the Stories We Don't Tell.

CPSIA information can be obtained
at www.ICGtesting.com
Printed in the USA
LVHW091259190221
679381LV00008B/699

9 781999 406790